MAIN BAD GUY

Also by **Nick Kolakowski**

A BRUTAL BUNCH OF HEARTBROKEN SAPS
SLAUGHTERHOUSE BLUES

BOISE LONGPIG HUNTING CLUB

A LOVE & BULLETS HOOKUP
BOOK THREE

MAIN
BAD
GUY

NICK KOLAKOWSKI

author of *SLAUGHTERHOUSE BLUES*

Main Bad Guy
Text copyright © 2019 Nick Kolakowski

Published by Shotgun Honey, an imprint of Down & Out Books

Shotgun Honey
PO Box 75272
Charleston, WV 25375
www.ShotgunHoney.com

Down & Out Books
3959 Van Dyke Rd, Ste. 265
Lutz, FL 33558
www.DownAndOutBooks.com

Cover Design by Bad Fido.

First Printing 2019

ISBN-10: 1-948235-70-6
ISBN-13: 978-1-948235-70-9

To G. and G.

MAIN BAD GUY

TWENTY YEARS AGO...

1

FIONA HAD BEEN AN HONOR STUDENT throughout school, a pig-tailed brown-noser who aced every test and kept her hand raised in class until it went numb. "I want to win everything," she always told her classmates, an attitude that would serve her well in adulthood—especially when she had to walk into rooms full of men with guns.

Under different circumstances, she might have become a neurosurgeon or a business executive. Instead, she met August Leadbetter, the self-styled Che Guevara of her eighth-grade class, and the best kisser in her life until she met Bill. (Every school has a few of those revolutionaries, to balance out the brown-nosers.)

August liked to leap on his desk and yell punk lyrics in class.

August stood on the roof of his mother's house on humid summer afternoons and tossed water balloons at the open sunroofs of passing cars, hoping to send a soaked and panicked driver off the road.

August also pushed little red pills. And Fiona was the experimental type, if you pressured her hard enough.

"Oh, come on," August said one afternoon, unzipping his pin-studded backpack to reveal his stash, most of it stolen from his mom's medicine cabinet. "It'll be fun. The world goes into slow motion. It's the only way to survive math class."

They stood behind the equipment shed at the far end of the football field, safe from prying eyes. Fiona extended a hand, fear prickling her belly—or maybe it was excitement. The pill in her palm seemed very large. She asked: "What if I overdose?"

"You only overdose if you mix drugs," August shot back. "Come on, it'll relax you. Exams are making you all stressed out."

Figuring you only live once (*carpe diem*, as her Latin teacher always said), Fiona popped that little bundle of chemicals in her mouth and swallowed, her throat clicking…

…and felt rain on her face.

The smell of the ocean filled her skull.

Opened her eyes—had she closed them?

She saw gray sky, black pines. She lay on something rough and cold. A dim roar filled her ears: the blood in her veins, amplified to superhuman decibels by whatever the fuck August had given her. No, wrong: the sound came from outside of her. Holy crap, she thought. Where am I?

She turned her head and saw a maroon station wagon barreling toward her.

Her confused brain burned two precious seconds wondering if the car was an illusion (the "drug talking," as the characters in novels always put it) and she was "tripping out" or whatever. Her hammering heart said no, she was a real person on a real road with a real mom-mobile about to squish her flat.

She thrashed, and her body flopped across the yellow line as the honking station wagon screeched to a stop three feet away. The driver's door opened, and a middle-aged lady with a pinched face burst out. Through the windshield Fiona saw a young kid staring at her slack-jawed, shocked. You and me both, she wanted to tell him. You and me both.

When she got back, she planned on murdering August in as painful a way as possible. Dunking him in a piranha tank seemed like just the thing. Or skewering him with a red-hot poker.

The lady yelled: "Are you okay?"

Fiona opened her mouth to speak and emitted only the softest of gurgles.

"Oh my God," the lady continued. "Are you on drugs?"

Fiona grunted like a bullfrog. Her legs and arms refused to peel from the pavement, no matter how hard she tensed her muscles. The lady hovered over her, and Fiona's roving eyes settled on something that sent a shivery bolt of fear through her gut: the station wagon's license plate.

It read: Delaware.

And Fiona had popped that pill in the great state of New Jersey.

Fear dumped enough adrenaline into her bloodstream to reactivate her knees. She stood on quaking legs, brushing away the lady's hand. Another car hummed to a stop behind the station wagon. Fiona could see something bulky on its roof, like a ski rack.

No, those were bubble lights, because it was a friggin' police car.

Well, today was going nowhere but up.

"This girl's on drugs," the lady yelled at the bored cop with a porn-star moustache who climbed out of the cruiser, his hand on his service pistol. As he hip-strutted toward them, Fiona pictured her parents' faces hard with disappointment, the school principal wagging a finger in her face, her science-club friends whispering behind her back. No top school would accept a girl with an arrest record. And getting a good job? Forget about it.

August had set her whole life on fire.

"What's your name, girl?" the cop asked, halting five feet away.

Keep up the zombie act, Fiona told herself. Make them think you're not a threat. Letting her chin droop to her collar, she shuffled a few steps to the left, trying to clear a little space between her and the adults.

"Kids these days," the lady continued. "I mean, it's not like we didn't have controlled substances in our day, officer, but from what I hear they're getting into now…"

The cop swiveled toward Mom of the Year, to better absorb her nuanced assessment of the nation's drug problem, and Fiona saw her chance. She sprinted for the cruiser, the cop shouting at her to stop, reaching for her—too late. She slammed the door and locked it before he could grab the handle. The keys were in the ignition, thank God.

As the cop pulled his baton from his belt, readying to smash the window, Fiona keyed the engine to life and pushed the column-shift and hit the gas, barreling down the road in reverse. The cop's baton smacked the hood as she passed. She giggled. It was like something out of a movie.

Now to deal with the problem at hand: escaping. She was tall for her age and had no problem seeing through the windshield. Her lifetime experience behind the wheel amounted to driving a pickup on the backroads of her cousin's farm, but she had watched enough action movies over the years to absorb how stuntmen executed a turnaround at speed, and it seemed simple enough. A hundred yards down the road, she stood on the brakes and spun the wheel, the view out the windows blurring, the cruiser tilting hard as it skidded onto the shoulder. Her heart froze. You've lost it, you idiot. You're going to crash.

But the cruiser bounced back to pavement, facing in the right direction. In the rearview mirror, the shrinking cop yelled into the radio on his shoulder, no doubt calling backup. Beside him, Mother of the Year clutched her jaw, swaying from foot to foot.

At least he didn't shoot at me, Fiona thought. The only thing worse than getting kicked out of school for drugs is a bullet to the head.

She accelerated to ninety, trying to put as much distance as possible between her and…what? They would scramble a fleet of cop cars to hunt her down, from all directions. Helicopters overhead, armed with snipers and spotlights, as the radio waves crackled with her name and description. So long as she stayed in this vehicle, nowhere was safe. You need a big parking lot. Like a mall or something. Dump the vehicle, call your father, and hide. At least you feel fine. Imagine if that pill had messed up your ability to walk.

Even as her brain puzzled over logistics, she found herself laughing uncontrollably. This was *fun*.

Three miles later, the road widened into four lanes, and the forest on either side of the road gave way to endless concrete: a sea of parking lots around the glittering island of a mega-mall. Some Dark God was protecting her. She steered the cruiser into the first open space she saw, locked it, and ran toward the mall, avoiding the front doors in favor of the loading docks in the rear.

Her joy at finding an ancient payphone on the mall's third floor curdled when she tapped her hip and realized, for the first time since waking up on the road, that her cute Paul

Frank monkey wallet was missing. Had that little shit August taken it?

Across from the payphone was an Irish pub, packed with hungry shoppers. Through the windows, she saw a family stand to leave, the father dropping a few bills and quarters in tip money on the table. Guilt squeezed her throat as she entered the pub and scooped up the change, ducking out the door before a waiter noticed. How long until the cops swept through the mall, on the hunt for a teenage carjacker?

"Get in the ladies' room," her father told her over the phone, once she explained everything that had happened. "In a stall. Wait. Don't leave for anybody or anything. I'll get there in exactly three hours from this moment, after it's dark. What's the back of the mall like?"

She wiped a tear from her cheek. "Like you'd expect. There's like the place where trucks come in, some dumpsters, stuff like that."

"I'll be by the dumpsters. You know the car."

"Okay, Daddy. I'm so sorry."

"Don't be sorry. Just get through it."

Her father was waiting where he promised. He still had his work beard, which made him look a bit like a young Fidel Castro. I guess it helps him blend in, Fiona thought. Wherever he's been going lately, it gives him a serious suntan. His sleeves had slid away from his wrists, revealing small cuts and a few nasty bruises.

When she slid into the front seat, he jabbed a thumb over his shoulder. She opened the rear door, and he said: "No. The trunk."

"Okay, okay," she said. "I'm sorry about what happened, but that's a pretty messed-up punishment."

"How else am I getting you past any cops?" he said.

But there were no checkpoints. Cocooned in the warm

darkness of the trunk, Fiona contemplated her wild day. Sure, it was a rush to score a hundred-ten on a test (she always went for the extra credit) or show off her math skills in front of the class, but that was nothing compared to the high-octane thrill of ripping off a police cruiser and taking it on a high-speed chase. The fear just added to the excitement. For the first time in her life, She wondered: who am I really?

Once they crossed into New Jersey, her father pulled the car onto the side of the road and let her out so she could ride in front. They sat in silence for the next fifty miles, Fiona chewing her nails and doing her best not stare at her father too closely.

After what seemed like an eternity, he asked: "So what happened?"

"A boy at school gave me a pill. I'm sorry I took it. I was stupid."

"You were curious." He smiled. "It's one of the best things about you. But you can't take a teenage boy at his word."

"I'm sorry."

"And I'm sure you'll never do it again. Did the cops identify you?"

She shook her head. "I didn't tell them my name. Didn't tell them anything."

"Good. And I bet they'll want to cover all this up. It doesn't reflect well on a department when a kid steals an officer's car. I'll make some calls, see if anyone's making an issue of it. If they are, well, someone down the line probably owes me a favor."

"Thank you." Relief swept through her like a warm wave. She added the mileage from the highway signs and figured her body had traveled some hundred-fifty miles south while her mind orbited Mars. At least she had done it (somehow) in a single afternoon; she could plead illness at school tomorrow. Her mother, working yet another epic shift at the hospital, would have no idea what happened, provided her father kept his mouth shut.

Fiona suspected he would. Her father never liked starting drama, and things had been powder-keg tense for a long time between her parents.

Her father's next question snapped her back to reality: "What was the boy's name?"

"August."

"What are you going to do to August?"

She lashed out a foot. "Hit him in the balls."

Her father shook his head. "No, sweetie, that's not good enough. You need to punch him in the face, not just once but repeatedly. You need to break his nose. Understand?"

"I don't want to hurt him for life. Or disfigure him."

"You're such a kind soul, hon." He squeezed her shoulder. "But if you break his nose, you're doing him a favor. For the rest of his life, every time he looks in the mirror, he'll remember what happened. The consequences of doing bad. So maybe the next time he wants to push drugs on someone, he'll think better of it."

It made sense. August might have killed her with that pill. If he did the same thing to someone else, and they died, how could she live with herself?

"In fact, when we get home, I have a gift for you." Her father smiled. "Something that might help you out with your friend."

The gift was a pair of brass knuckles. Her father taught her how to hit with the added weight on her hand, using one of his worn-out punching bags in the garage. He demonstrated proper technique with his own steel knuckle-dusters, which had a little spike on the pinkie edge ("It's for opening beer bottles," he joked). They had a weekend of real father-daughter bonding before he had to leave again.

The next time August saw her behind the shed, between fourth period and lunch, his eyes sparkled with relief. "Thank God," he cried, arms spreading wide for the hug. "I don't know why the hell you wandered off like that…"

She hit him hard in the face, twisting her hips like her father taught her. The brass knuckles crunched the delicate bones around his nose, and blood flew. She let him fall to his knees without punching him again; her father might have advocated crippling someone who crossed you, but Fiona figured she would show August a little mercy. After all, he had given her the most exciting afternoon of her teenage life.

"Why did you do that?" August blubbered through his bloody hands. "You're nice."

"You have no idea who I am," Fiona said, wiping the brass knuckles on her jeans. She didn't know who she was, either; not really. But she intended to find out.

THIS PAST MONDAY

1

THEY WERE HALFWAY TO THE AIRPORT when the big black car tried to kill them.

Out of the corner of her eye, Fiona saw it swerving across three lanes of highway, its fender aimed at their cab's rear panel. Classic pursuit intervention technique, beloved by cops the world over. No time to scream. She had her seat-belt buckled, as she always did in cars. She grabbed Bill by the shoulder, pulling him toward her, her arms cradling his neck and head.

Their cabbie never saw it coming. He was too busy talking about making a fortune in real estate, through some scheme involving credit cards and home equity loans. Fiona loved how everyone in New York had a hustle. The cabbie's last words ("I'm paying the mortgage, *double-time*, okay?") were inter-rupted by the mighty crunch of steel on steel, and his head smacked the scratched plastic partition between the front and back seats, painting it red, as the cab flipped onto its side.

Bill's heavy body crashed into Fiona, blasting the air out

her lungs. Her face pressed against the cracked window, gravel on the other side—they had stopped on the shoulder. She smelled gas and scorched rubber, felt a slick warmth on her back. She was cut, but how bad?

"Haven't we suffered *enough*?" Bill braced his feet against the partition, levering his body away from her.

Wincing at the ache in her ribs, Fiona unbuckled her seatbelt and twisted around until her legs were under her, feet flat on the window. She stood, pressed tight against Bill, their heads a few inches below the door that had become their ceiling. She reached behind her back and felt the source of the blood trickling into her waistband: a clean laceration to the right of her spine, long but not deep. Her shirt would staunch the bleeding until she could slap a bandage on it. Hopefully.

Stuffing a hand through the broken cash hole in the partition, Bill stabbed two fingers into the driver's bloody neck. "I think this dude died, dear."

"Losing half your skull tends to do that." Fiona drew her pistol and checked that the safety was on. "Cover your eyes."

Bill did as he was told. Gritting her teeth, Fiona reversed the pistol in her grip and smashed it against the window one, two, three times until it shattered into a gummy mess, each blow sending fresh pain down her arm. Using the pistol-barrel as a rake, she swept the broken glass from the window-frame, then poked her head into the open air. Nobody took a shot at her. Traffic along the highway had already slowed, dozens of faces gawping at her through windshields.

The black car was nowhere in sight.

That was weird. What kind of professional didn't confirm the kill?

"Get the bag," she said, pushing through the window. Her every joint and tendon begged for mercy: too many weeks on the road, too many fights, too many tumbles and punches and falls. The cab rocked under her weight, threatening to tip over. She stood, arms out, surfing it as she sought a good place to jump.

"Ma'am, yes, ma'am," Bill shouted, and their bag sailed out the window. Because it was filled with lumps of gold, it flew only a few feet before thudding onto the white strip that separated the shoulder from the roadway. Fiona leapt after it, ears pricked for sirens.

It took Bill a little more effort to squeeze free of the cab. He jumped and stumbled hard, hands flailing for balance. Fiona already had the bag looped over her shoulder, its strap biting into her bruised flesh. She needed to call their contact at the airport, the man who would have changed their gold into cash for a hefty premium. Plans had changed. The new plan was hiding out and staying alive.

Dragging Bill upright, she led him toward the small thicket of elms beyond the shoulder. Her body felt like a crumpled soda can, everything bent and broken, her pulse too loud in her ears. How much longer could they go before she collapsed?

"I'm done with this shit," she told Bill as they ran. "We need out of this life."

2

THE DEAN WAS PISSED.

Or pissing, if you wanted to get technical about it.

"You might think this is barbaric," he said, unzipping his fly. "But trust me, the desecration is appropriate to the situation."

Having justified his actions to God and man, the Dean unleashed a spray on the thick Persian rug, swirling his hips as if trying to scrawl his signature in urine. He whistled a song through clenched teeth, tuneless and off-key. His dark-suited men, lining the walls on either side of him, struggled heroically not to laugh.

At the enormous desk behind the Dean, Simon also fought to keep his expression neutral. His round sunglasses helped, but it was hard to keep his lips from peeling into a snarl. He busied himself with lighting a cigarette, telling himself: best to let this *pizdá* get it out of his system. I can always have a rug cleaned, and a war is something I don't need right now.

The Dean shook out his last drops, zipped up his fly, and

swiveled on his heel. His eyes blazed with fury. From the jacket of his herringbone suit he drew a thin cigar, bit the tip, and spat a wet nub of tobacco at the silver bowl on a nearby table. "Now," he said, patting his pockets for a lighter or matches. "Where was I?"

"You were blaming me for Fiona and Bill," Simon said.

"Yes, and you didn't seem to be *empathizing* properly, so I made an example of your rug." The Dean, finding no fire for his cigar, snapped his fingers for Simon's gold lighter on the desk. "Fiona comes to the city, asks for your help, and you not only give it to her, but you neglect to tell me?"

"I don't work for you." Simon blew a smoke ring, making no move to hand over the lighter. "You and I are business partners, out of convenience. And your conflicts are not mine."

"That's what you think." The Dean took the seat across from Simon. "Speaking honestly, when Bill first stole that money from me, and Fiona joined him, I pictured it as a small issue. Just send men with guns."

"A straightforward solution. How many has she killed?" Simon asked.

"Enough to give me heartburn." The Dean began to reach for Simon's lighter, and stopped. It was clear from his expression that he wanted Simon to hand it over, to complete this little power game. When Simon crossed his arms and leaned back, smoke trickling from the corner of his mouth, the Dean's cheeks reddened.

"It's not easy replacing men with guns," the Dean continued, adjusting his collar. "Not like you can go online and just order more, two-day shipping, satisfaction guaranteed. And now Fiona and Bill are back in the city, merrily wrecking things left and right, which just draws attention to us. You included."

"I am not concerned," Simon said. "What bothers me is,

how you discovered she came to me."

"We have eyes everywhere. Who crashed a car into her cab?"

"Excuse me?"

"Someone rammed her taxi off the highway. Not long ago. We have the video. Security camera on a building nearby." The Dean frowned. "Fiona and Bill ran off. They're hurt, albeit not badly enough for my tastes."

Simon shook his head, wondering (not for the first time) what kind of man used words like 'albeit' in everyday speech. "Fiona and Bill make enemies like a dog picks up fleas."

"Well, it wasn't my men who crashed into her." The Dean, rather than suffer the indignity of begging for a light, chomped the unlit cigar. "So, who the hell did?"

Simon shrugged.

"Our purchased cop, he said the cab was on an airport run. They're trying to get out of town." The Dean laughed. "We have people at every airport, and Penn and Grand Central, and as many subways as we can cover. We will expose those cockroaches to the light, given enough time. Keep that in mind if she reaches out to you again."

"I'll remember my rug," Simon said. "Hundred dollars per square foot."

"As if you didn't have the funds to repair it." The Dean pointed the cigar at the lacquered woods and gold-leaf highlights of Simon's office, the antique furniture, the ornate paintings hanging on the walls. "Fiona appears, you tell me. No equivocations, no prevarication. Understood?"

Simon stubbed out his cigarette in the ashtray by his elbow and lit a fresh one. His next smoke ring drifted into the Dean's face. "I understand perfectly," he said, stuffing the lighter in his pocket.

The Dean's cheeks colored heart-attack purple. "Fine," he

hissed through a tight throat. Slipping his unsmoked cigar into his vest, he stood and marched for the door, his men falling into line behind him. "Otherwise, this all ends in tears for you."

3

WALKER SPENT A FEW DAYS in a trailer-park motel on the rim of Hudson Bay, seventy loonies a week for a double-wide at the very edge of the property where the mud and gravel gave way to pine woods filled with trash. The sun never set. It was a white-hot lance that pierced through the frayed curtains at all hours, keeping him awake despite the beer and pills, and after two miserable days he took refuge in the windowless bathroom, finally dozing in the shower stall atop a sheet.

On the third bright night he walked into the trailer near the front gate that served as an office, on the hunt for aluminum foil to cover his windows. The old lady behind the desk ignored him, her faded blue eyes locked on the small television in the far corner. The screen trembled with images of fire, dead bodies under white sheets, an Elvis costume riddled with holes. The footage cut to a mugshot of a suspect: a young woman with raven-dark hair, smirking for the camera. Then another police-precinct portrait: a handsome man with a heavy jaw and black hair streaked with gray, his face beginning to soften with age.

He knew the couple. Without a word he dropped into the plastic seat beside the door, and the old lady silently poured him a juice-glass full of whiskey from her stash beneath the register. They sat and drank and watched as the newscaster described a trail of murder and thievery from Oklahoma to Nicaragua to New York City.

Once they finished the bottle he returned to his trailer and shrugged on his canvas jacket over his frayed t-shirt and pocketed his last two hundred loonies in cash. He had no passport, no driver's license, no phone, no cards. The old lady offered a limp wave when he opened her door just long enough to toss the keys on her desk.

A single call to the States would have summoned someone to retrieve him. Instead he walked down the two-lane that led from the trailer park to the logging town at the bottom of the valley, his steel-toed boots clicking on the pavement. The inside of his head felt bruised and his stomach boiled with acid, but every breath filled him with new life.

The town had one convenience store, where he bought a bus ticket to Montreal and waited the ninety minutes until it arrived on the bench outside, sipping a jumbo cup of black coffee. Nobody spoke to him. His white beard was a grimy thicket and his eyes were hard. He kept imagining people blown to black clouds, all their flesh and dreams drifting from a gunmetal sky.

In Montreal the bus dropped him on Rue Saint-Denis, beside a strip of upscale bars and a cat café. This far south, at this time of year, the sun set after nine, darkness comforting him like a warm blanket as he stood on the sidewalk rotating his neck, popping his joints, bending to touch his toes. He played an invisible piano to loosen his hands. His time up north had helped clean his blood and clear his head, but he worried about his reflexes, his gift for shifting a mark's attention.

He also needed a place to lay low, and something to eat. From his previous stay in the city he knew there was a sculpture garden at the bottom of Saint-Denis where the junkies had a sleeping-bag colony. A couple decades ago he might have taken that option, fought for a strip of cardboard beneath an overhang. Now he needed to renew his strength for the days ahead and that meant a clean bed, a door with locks, new clothes, and a shower hot enough to boil away the dirt crusting his skin.

His first stop was the loudest watering hole he could find, a sweaty box stuffed with screaming college kids. Dark, no security cameras, a bored lump of a bouncer more interested in chatting up underage girls than watching the door. Perfect. He made one pass, departing through the rear exit ten minutes later with a pair of stolen wallets in his pockets, fat with bills and credit cards, and a shiny phone swiped from a coat. So far, so good.

The phone's SIM card he dumped in the alley. At an all-night market he used one of the credit cards to purchase a razor, a pair of steel barber scissors, athletic tape, a prepaid SIM, and a handful of gift cards. He remembered his nephew telling him about the orange pills that everyone in his unit popped to stay awake on night missions in Iraq, their blood humming electric as they swept villages and kicked down doors. He wished for a handful of those bright little babies, which were probably a lot cleaner than the pills he had swallowed in Vietnam, but caffeine and sugar would have to do.

Next door to the market, a fast-food joint served poutine to a crowd of happy drunks. He locked himself in one of its two bathrooms and hacked off the beard and shaved the stubble, ignoring the fists banging on the metal door. After he finished, he slipped the barber scissors down his sleeve, hidden by his jacket and held in place by his watchband, retrievable in an instant. He popped the prepaid SIM card into the stolen phone, slipped the tape and gift cards into his jacket pockets, and dumped everything else in the trash, along with the credit card he used at the market.

Exiting the bathroom, he waited his turn at the counter and ordered a jumbo coffee, plus an extra-large basket of fries and cheese curds. Despite the crowd he found an open stool beside the window, with a good angle on the street. Chewing and sipping, he wondered about his next move. How long since you really hustled at street level? Nine, ten years? I don't know the new traps. The ways they can sniff you out. How fast they can nail you. It's so tempting to not cross the border. But family is family.

A whiff of perfume like wet candy, the fission of someone invading his airspace. Turning his head, he found himself nearly nose-to-nose with a girl in fishnet stockings and black-rimmed glasses. "Hey, old guy," she said. "What's your name?"

He tilted away from her, curious about the chemical making her pupils vibrate at such a high frequency. "Walker," he said.

"Walker, you leaving anytime soon? Because we'd like your seat." She nodded toward a strapping young man standing a few feet away, his arms slabbed with muscle, a poutine basket in each hand.

"I'm not done yet," Walker said, lifting his half-empty coffee.

The girl was having none of it. Placing her open purse on the counter beside his gravy-spattered basket, she said: "That's okay. We can just share your space. Right, Rog?"

Rog seemed unsure. He locked eyes with Walker and

took a step sideways, mumbling about finding another seat.

Walker shrugged and shifted his gaze to the window. A soft man in a good suit leaned against a streetlamp, bent at the waist, and vomited a greenish muck on the sidewalk. The crowd moaned and laughed at the spectacle. The suited man straightened, spat, and commenced a zombie-like shuffle down the street. It gave Walker an idea.

A fist poked his ribs. The girl punching him, not hard enough to hurt. A violation nonetheless. Walker stood and she hit him again, in the sternum this time, biting her lip with the effort. "Time to go," she said. "Get your ancient ass out of here."

No point in trying to reason with this surly space alien. Instead Walker lifted his coffee cup and upended it into the girl's purse, filling it to the brim.

"Now I'm through," he said.

The girl screamed and shoved past him, fishing her phone and keys from the drenched ruin. The restaurant frozen silent, thirty pairs of eyes memorizing his face, his clothes, the way he moved. There I go again, Walker mused. Too impulsive for my own good. Heading for the door, he jabbed a finger in Rog's stunned face. "Trade up," he told the kid.

Outside again, a little anxious about cops, he followed the suited man around the far corner. Down a residential street of quiet houses, lit dimly. Walker slipped close, the acid stink of vomit and cheap beer making his nostrils flare, and executed his gentlest sleeper hold. The man grunted, hands thrashing against Walker's forearms like anxious birds, before slumping into unconsciousness.

Walker dragged the wheezing body into a nearby alley and propped it against a wall. Rifling through the suit pockets, he found a key-fob. He walked down the street, pressing the button on the fob until a late-model Audi honked in response.

In the trunk he found a dark blue suit in a bag, roughly his size, and a striped button-down shirt. A road-kit with a flashlight and some flares. So far, so good.

The Audi's booming engine carried him back down Rue Saint-Denis and over the river and onto the highways ringing the city. On the satellite radio he found a channel playing heavy metal, not something he usually liked, but it would serve as a little aural caffeine for the trip. He gave up on the idea of a soft bed in Canada. Better at this point to keep moving south. Turning on his new phone, he dialed a number he knew by heart.

4

THE DOGS IN THE KENNELS snarled and barked. The one closest to Fiona, a gray pit bull with one eye and a scarred flank, jabbed its nose between the wires of its cage. She offered the animal a fist to lick, and it calmed down.

"After we're done, I need you out of here," Trevor said, snapping on a pair of surgical gloves. The smudges under his eyes suggested the tail end of a long shift. He was a vet trying to work his way from under nine years of school debt, which always made him more than happy to help Fiona—for a price.

"Understood," she said, peeling off her bloody shirt. Bill, standing behind her, slipped a playful finger under the elastic band of her sports bra. She slapped his hand away. "Just wait until your shirt's off," she told him. "We'll get a poke at those man-boobs."

"I'm serious," Trevor said, plucking alcohol wipes from the container beside the sink. "I got guys coming in and out of here all the time, needing help. One of them sees you, I

28

have a real problem."

"You won't tell anyone we were here," Fiona said, her tone flat. "It'll just make things rougher for you. Someone might do some Reservoir Dogs shit."

"I'm just trying to keep the bailiff away from the door." Stepping close enough to see the bruises and cuts marking Fiona's torso, Trevor whistled softly. "They really did a number on you, didn't they?"

"You should have seen the other lady," Bill said, extending his hand to the gray pit bull, which bared its fangs and growled.

"If you have some super-glue," Fiona said, "I can take care of my smaller cuts. But my ribs are really busted up from a fight, and I have a bigger cut on my back that feels like it's about to rip open again. Just patch me up best you can."

"This is really going to cost you." Trevor opened drawers beneath the table where Fiona sat, retrieving packs of bandages, a pre-loaded skin-stapler, tweezers, and a bottle of hydrogen peroxide. "The Dean, the Rockaway Mob put a huge price on your head, plus the cops want you, and who knows who else? It's a lot of heat."

Fiona unzipped the bag beside her and pulled out a small lump of gold, placing it on the table beside her hip. "This should cover it," she said. "It's more than the Dean pays people for information. Don't ask where I got it."

Trevor squinted at the precious metal. "What are those white flecks?"

"Bits of Nazi teeth," Bill said. "Let your imagination fill in the rest."

"Not the weirdest coin I've been paid in, believe me," Trevor said, unfurling the stethoscope around his neck and placing its disk against Fiona's back. After listening to her breathing, he probed her bruised ribs with the tips of his fingers. "This hurts a lot, right?"

Fiona bit her lip, hissing: "No, feels wonderful."

"Good news is, doesn't feel like anything's broken," Trevor said. "But you need to heal. How many days can you rest?"

"How about none?" Fiona said. "None sounds about right."

Trevor swabbed the cuts on her back with alcohol wipes. "I'm serious. Fortunately for you, it doesn't seem like anything's infected, but the longer you keep moving, the more you'll wear down. If you don't choose to rest, your body will make you rest."

"We'll figure something out," Bill said, patrolling the edges of the examination room. He peeked into the empty hallway and the reception area beyond. Trevor's veterinary practice was a small one, squeezed between a liquor store and a Tibetan restaurant, and supposedly there were no more appointments today. The front door was locked. So why did Bill suddenly feel so paranoid?

"I heard you fled down to South America," Trevor said, slipping bandages over Fiona's smaller wounds.

"Who told you that?" Fiona asked.

Trevor shrugged. "Every desperado coming in here to get patched up. You're legends. Said you caused some chaos in Oklahoma, too. Killed some cops?"

"Bill let himself get seduced by some little slattern outside of Tulsa," Fiona said. "The town bartender, of all people. Her cannibal relatives would have buried him in the chicken coop if I hadn't shown up."

"Hey," Bill said. "That lady drugged me. I was helpless."

"A likely story." Fiona grinned at him. "Then we went south for a little while. Not all the way to South America, but pretty close. We're back because we needed money, and someone had a gig for us."

"That's where the gold comes from, I assume." Trevor picked up the stapler. "That bigger cut in your lower back, it's clotted up, but that won't hold. I'm going to staple it, okay?"

"What's one more scar?" Fiona said, biting her lip. "Do it."

Bracing his free hand against her spine, Trevor pressed the stapler to her flesh and snapped seven staples across the wound, closing it tight. Then he applied alcohol and a fresh bandage. "Reminds me of school," he said, with a slight smile.

"I remember your hands always shook when you patched me up," she said. "They're steady now."

"Well, I was a dumb kid back in the day." He slid his hand up her back. "In more ways than one."

Fiona glanced at Bill in the doorway, his attention still focused on the reception area. She flicked her head at Trevor, not unkind. He nodded and removed his hand, snapping his gloves into the trash as he moved to the sink. He asked: "What's your plan?"

"Better you don't know," she said. "Just in case."

Trevor shrugged, scrubbed his fingers, and slipped on new gloves. "Yeah, just in case someone threatens to pull my tongue out. Bill, you ready? Let me examine those bruises."

Bill's cheekbones had swollen so much, he feared looking at himself in the mirror. He felt an absurd jealousy for action-movie heroes who could emerge from a pummeling with only a photogenic cut or two on their brow. In real life, skin behaved like ripe fruit when you hit it.

"I'm okay," Bill said, glancing at Fiona. "Nothing that won't heal."

Fiona rolled her eyes. "Give it up, tough guy. I didn't mean the man-boob comment."

"These are pecs," Bill said, slapping his chest. "Nothing but muscle here." With that, he stepped toward the exam table, which might have saved his life.

A metal flower popped open on the doorjamb, near where he had stood before. A loud crack echoed through the reception area.

Fiona hit the floor, pulling Trevor with her. Bill joined them, landing beside a hot lump of metal: a spent bullet, big. The dogs howled in fear.

Fiona's hand tightened on Trevor's collar until it cut into his throat. "Did you tell anyone?"

Trevor shook his head and moaned. "I've been in your sight the whole time."

The dogs paced and howled, saliva dripping from their jaws. The gray pit bull threw itself against the cage door, desperate to break free. Crawling on elbows and knees, Bill peeked into the reception area: still empty. A cracked hole dead-center in the smoked glass of the front door.

"Bill?" Fiona asked. "Who's coming in?"

Still on his stomach, Bill edged into the hallway until he could see through the wide window to the left of the door. The sidewalk was empty, and so was the street beyond. "Nobody," he said.

Fiona groaned. "What the hell?"

"I bet it's our buddy from the highway," Bill said. "Messing with us."

"The back door, it's past the other exam room," Trevor offered.

"We can take a hint, dear." Fiona released his collar. "But before we go, I'm helping myself to some of your doggie painkillers, okay? And your phone. And a t-shirt that's not covered in my blood."

SULLY WAS A SECOND-GENERATION pot farmer who dressed the part: faded denim jacket over a black hoodie, hiking boots clotted with drying soil, work-pants with big pockets. His blonde moustache, carefully waxed into whorls, gave his face a whimsical air, but Walker knew him as one of the hardest men between Burlington and Boston, which was saying something. The remains of more than a few enemies had fertilized Sully's secret fields over the years.

For this late-night meeting with Walker, Sully had selected a cozy flatbread restaurant at the end of Burlington's St. Paul Street, by the water. They sat in a dim booth beneath an antique poster for tractor parts, Sully with a micro-brew in front of him, Walker nursing a cup of black coffee. Walker wore the suit and shirt from the Audi's trunk, the pants a little short but otherwise a perfect fit.

Sully drained his beer, spotting his elaborate moustache with foam. "Didn't expect you this soon," he said.

"Got business south," Walker said, trying to leave it at

that.

"Don't get me wrong, it's always good seeing a friendly face, even one as ugly as yours," Sully said, not laughing. "But in my line of work, I don't like unexpected things."

"We're not in business together," Walker said. "You're just holding my stuff, remember?"

"Oh, yeah. For no money."

Walker smiled without warmth. "Good thing we're friends."

"I know I owed you a favor, but after this, we're settled, okay? You talk to your other old friends lately?"

"Which old friends?"

Sully shrugged. "Fed friends?"

"No," Walker said. "They're unpleasant people. You got what's mine?"

Sully studied him, still holding his empty beer glass, until Walker snapped his fingers twice.

"Chill out," Sully said, eyebrows raised.

"I am chill."

"No, chill people aren't rude. When you're in the weed business, you know tension in all its varieties. If the Feds talked to me, I'd be tense, too."

"I think your weed's making you paranoid." Walker leaned close, squinting. "You know I stopped working for them years ago. I got sick of their business."

"But they still call you from time to time, right?"

"What's up with you?"

"Couple of my guys just got snatched up. Merchandise disappeared. Then you come around. It's been an odd week. You said you came from Montreal?"

"That's what I told you." Walker slapped the table.

"What'd I say? Chill. We're just talking. Border's locked down. How'd you get over?"

"Walked."

"You didn't bribe nobody?"

"Didn't see anybody."

"Walked through the woods?"

"You see my shoes?" Walker had parked the Audi on the shoulder of a gravel road two miles from the border, used the flashlight from the trunk to guide his way into the United States. His feet sinking ankle-deep in mud, mosquitos dive-bombing his neck, the bagged suit on his arm snagging on branches. The fantasy of a cool bed and a hot shower powering him through the dark.

Sully craned his neck so he could see beneath the table. "Better get those polished up."

Walker shrugged. A few miles south of the border, he had slipped onto a farm near the road and stolen a mountain bike from an unlocked barn, leaving a wad of loonies and one of the gift cards behind. The less Sully knew about his choices in transportation, the better.

"Anyway, I'm impressed." Sully leaned forward, close enough for Walker to smell prime weed seeping from the man's pores. "I tried the same thing once, just to see what would happen. I picked this big stretch of forest north of here, nobody around for miles. Or so I imagined. I park the car and hike until the map on my phone tells me I'm on the Canadian side, then I turn around and come back. Thirty seconds after I cross over, these border-patrol dudes show up on ATVs, yelling that I'm in the States. I was like, 'I realize that, gentlemen.' They would've thrown my ass in jail if I hadn't started waving my driver's license and saying I'd gotten lost, it was all a mistake, sorry."

"How do you think they found you?"

"Who knows? Drones, heat sensors, whatever. There's no more privacy in the world."

Walker made a big show of keeping his hands flat on the table, bracketing his coffee cup. Trying to project an aura of zero threat. "Cool story, brother. Listen, I just want my stuff."

"You'll get what's yours. Why all the nervousness? You're fancy-free on U.S. soil. Where you staying tonight?"

"Just a house. Not far from here. And not for long."

"You should have a beer. Coffee wires you up."

"Got miles to go before I sleep."

"Couple lines of poetry will definitely get you right laid around these parts. The grad students pop right open for a gangster who knows his verse. One of the better perks of living in Vermont. If you talked to the Feds, it's okay. Doesn't mean anything."

"How many times I got to tell you?"

Sully stroked his moustache. "That wasn't a 'no.'"

Walker pulled up his shirt, revealing a pale torso etched with scars. "You see a wire? I'm not a snitch."

"Listen now, I'm not implying anything." Sully raised his hands in mock surrender.

"Why don't you chill out?" Walker tucked his shirt back in. As he shifted his left wrist, the scissors pressed cool and sharp against his skin. At the table to their right sat Sully's usual security, a pair of hefty types in unassuming fleece and jeans, an untouched fennel-sausage flatbread between them. Too much weight for Walker to handle, hidden knife or no.

"I am sub-zero," Sully said. "If you want your stuff, sure, I got it right here." Reaching slowly into his unzipped hoodie, he retrieved the slim manila envelope that Walker had given him earlier that year, passed it under the table.

"Thanks," Walker said, tucking the envelope into his jacket pocket.

"Can I ask you something?"

"Yes."

"What's your business south?"

"Family." With a wink, Walker drained his coffee cup and stood. The normalcy of this place—the tables packed with university types, the bustling waitstaff, the blazing clay oven—made him tense, his nerves crackling. Or maybe it was the caffeine he kept mainlining. Or maybe it was the knowledge that, once he left here, paranoid Sully would almost certainly try to kill him. Why had he trusted his stuff to this whackjob?

Headed out the restaurant's front door, Walker glanced over his shoulder and saw Sully's grim men already out of their seats, their hands in their pockets. On the sidewalk he hooked left, around the corner that led to the parking lot.

Sully always spent top dollar on the best muscle, ex-military types who would sweep the zone quick and careful, giving Walker precious few chances for an ambush. Not that he had any intention of committing suicide by taking them on, but their caution might buy him a little more time to escape.

A pair of lamps bolted to the restaurant's roof cast a pale glow over five rows of parked cars. Nobody in sight. With just a few seconds before the muscle rounded the corner, Walker settled on a late-model BMW in the middle of the nearest row. He slammed his elbow into the driver's side window until it crunched into a milky cataract. The car's alarm blared, headlights flashing in panic.

He ducked and ran to the far end of the row, stopping beside a battered blue SUV with a fading 'Feel the Bern' sticker on the back window. Pressing his palms against the rear bumper, he bounced until the alarm kicked off, joining the BMW in wailing chorus.

Stooped low, breathing hard, he retreated to the fifth row, where the light and pavement ended in shadowy trees.

Dropping to his hands and knees beside a truck, cheek almost pressed against the cold gravel, he spied two pairs of hiking boots swiveling on the far side of the BMW. If they saw him now, they would kill him, alarms or no.

The restaurant's rear door crashed open, ejecting a swarm of line cooks in splattered whites. Flashing their onion-flecked knives, they howled in Spanish at Sully's men, who raised their hands and retreated the way they had come.

Walker had already ducked into the woods, angling for the dirt path that led to the lake, and the large pine where he had propped his bike. As he stepped through the underbrush, the envelope in his jacket pocket tapped gently against his ribs. A car key, a padlock key, a driver's license under yet another name, a clean credit card with a ten-thousand-dollar limit: he hoped that Sully had left it all alone.

I was an idiot to trust him, Walker cursed as he pulled the bike free of the branches. A guy so paranoid, he probably thinks an FBI midget is snorkeling in his toilet-tank. Just because an associate buries some bodies for you over the years doesn't make him your lifelong buddy. You're slipping, old man. You're slipping.

6

THE REAR OF TREVOR'S CLINIC opened onto a narrow alley with high brick walls. Fiona crouched in the doorway, her eyes locked on the opening to the street. In her experience, you put a bullet through someone's front door if you wanted to flush them out the back, into an ambush. But if the shooter was the same person who smashed into their cab on the highway, they were displaying a stunning lack of follow-through.

"Maybe we have a secret crush," Bill said, "and they're showing it in a really odd way."

"Hey, there's nothing odd about it." Fiona paused to draw her pistol, keeping it pressed tight against her leg. "There's nothing more romantic than a car crash."

"You scare me sometimes, dear. Especially with that shirt."

On their way out the door, Trevor had tossed Fiona an old t-shirt from a drawer, light blue with the words 'YOU CAN'T BUY LOVE, BUT YOU CAN ADOPT IT' on the front in comic sans. The back featured a black paw-print with the name of a local pet-adoption agency beneath. Hey, at least it was clean. Reaching back to squeeze Bill's knee, Fiona said: "At least it doesn't read, 'I'm with stupid.'"

"You're a laugh riot." Bill sighed. "Seriously, who'd we piss off this time?"

"Zero idea," she said. "And that's what freaks me out. I like to know who's shooting at me."

"Let me have Trevor's phone?"

"In my back pocket."

Bill gave Fiona a friendly pinch as he extracted the device. While he tapped and swiped the screen, Trevor tried quieting down the barking dogs. She felt a little guilty about barging in on him, sure, but what were ex-boyfriends for?

At least Trevor had done a fine job of patching her up. Three doggie painkillers dampened her sharper pains to dull aches, and the staples in her back pinched only a little when she straightened her spine. "You better not be checking your email," Fiona said.

"Just updating my Facebook status," Bill chuckled. "I'm writing, 'Back in New York, hunted by my old boss, anyone want to hang?' Seemed like the right time for it."

"Stop."

"I'm looking up that luxury condo over on Vernon," Bill said. "Remember all the news about it? The neighbors were protesting? I think construction got shut down while they paid off whoever needs paying off."

"Why don't we just steal a car? Get out of the city?"

"With everyone right on our ass? And if we get clear, what's next? Find some small town and hide out? I'm done with small towns." Bill flipped the phone so she could see the screen, and the image of an iron finger extending into a blue sky: a half-constructed high rise, its massive girders draped with orange mesh like a Christo art installation. "Name me another big place on this side of the river that's empty like this. We can rest, make some calls, whatever."

Fiona chewed the inside of her cheek. "I bet there's a guard on-site," she said. "Someone to stop people from coming in and ripping the wiring out of the walls."

"We sneak past him, take a high floor," Bill said. "Easy to defend, nobody around, no cops. Trust me, where else we going to find that in New York City?"

Fiona took the phone back, flicked open a map. "We'll walk there. Subway's too much of a box for me."

"Sure, that's fine." Bill hefted the bag, its gold softly clinking. "This is real light."

"Think of it as a really good workout."

At the mouth of the alley they stopped again so Fiona could peer around the corner. The sidewalk in front of Trevor's door was still empty—not unusual for a side-street in Queens in the late afternoon, but it made Fiona wonder if any bystanders had heard the shot and taken cover. Or called the police.

Heart pounding, she gestured for Bill to follow her, then walked south, toward the water. It was a bit of a hike to Vernon Boulevard, if they stuck to residential streets. Bill was in full paranoid mode, eyes flicking to every window and passing car, which made her feel safe enough to dial Simon from Trevor's phone. Her other hand stayed in her pocket, on her pistol.

That familiar growl answered on the fourth ring. "Yes?"

"It's me," she said. "Fiona."

Her phone beeped, the call dropping. Fiona pulled it away from her face, confused, and saw four bars of signal. Had Simon hung up on her?

"What happened?" Bill asked.

"I don't know," Fiona said. "If he doesn't want to talk to me…"

"Bad sign. Hold on a second." Raising a finger for her to wait, Bill disappeared inside a small convenience store on the corner, soon reappearing with two baseball caps and two pairs of sunglasses. "Look at these badass accessories. We're masters of disguise now."

Fiona mimed sticking two fingers down her throat. "Could you have picked any team other than the frigging Mets?"

"I just grabbed the first ones I saw." Bill grinned. "I swear, I didn't deliberately pick a team you hated with a fiery passion."

"Piss-poor disguise, anyway," Fiona said, slipping on the sunglasses and tucking her hair beneath the cap. "Any cop will see right through this."

Before Bill could respond, Fiona's phone buzzed, flashing an unknown number. She answered, hoping it wasn't one of Trevor's idiot friends. "Yeah?"

When Simon spoke, a crowd murmured behind him, punctuated by a honking horn. He sounded irate, his accent thicker than usual: "Are you a child?"

"Okay, I'm sorry for calling you direct," she said. "My back's in a corner."

"So is mine," he said. "I am on a burner, on the street, surrounded by the cowards and ingrates who make up the public. That is to say, I have a mole in my crew, reporting to the Dean. You didn't make it to the airport."

"That's right. Someone hit us on the highway."

"You know who?"

"No idea."

"It wasn't the Dean. He knew about the crash, thanks to a security camera. How many police are on his payroll, you think?"

"Not as many as he would like, fortunately. You tell him I

was meeting your gold guy at the airport?"

"No, and he has people at the airports, so your attacker may have done you a favor." A click, a loud exhale as Simon lit a cigarette. "You still owe me some money."

"Sure, I got it right here," she said. "It was a good little score."

Next to her, Bill offered an arched eyebrow.

"A good little score, but not a stealthy one." Simon chuckled. "You are all over the news, dear. Every channel, plus whatever the Internet does. The thing with the Tesla was particularly colorful. I am old enough to remember when a decapitation in Manhattan was not a newsworthy event."

"We'll pay you more if you help us."

Simon coughed, and Fiona pictured him blasting plumes of smoke out his nostrils. "As much as I would like to, my dear, I am in the bind. The Dean is watching everything. You're the bit of meat stuck in his tooth, irritating him to rage. He will spare no expense to put your head in a cardboard box on his desk."

"Well, he hasn't succeeded so far. If you can't help us, how are you getting your money?"

Simon fell silent long enough for Fiona to wonder if she had gone too far, dangling a threat like that. Through the line she heard a kid hollering, and the rumble of a truck. When Simon spoke again, his voice was gentle, the words paced. "I've always cared about you, Fiona. Not like a father, because you already have one of those. But because you're a different cut of criminal. Smarter, efficient. You wouldn't deny me what's mine."

"You're right," she said. "I wouldn't. Just make sure none of your people help the Dean, please?"

"I have no intention of allowing any of my people to assist that intellectual." Simon spat the last word. "I'll kill him at the first right opportunity. Now stay alive until you can pay me." With that last bit of encouragement, he hung up.

Slipping her phone back into her pocket, Fiona told Bill: "Went fine. Couldn't you tell?"

"Absolutely."

Heading south, Fiona found her thoughts drifting to Trevor. Not the worst relationship: he had been kind, funny, not terrible in the sack. They had rented an apartment together off-campus, their only tension stemming from Fiona's refusal to tell him how she paid her share of the rent. One night, four glasses of wine gave Trevor courage enough to stammer: *You're not doing sex work, are you?* Rather than take offense, she had laughed and kissed him on the forehead and said: *Of course not, silly.* She neglected to mention how she was making a thousand dollars a week as a courier, transporting packages between an ever-changing cast of Shady Dudes.

Things had come to a head when a skinny freak kicked open the front door of their apartment, intent on finding where Fiona had delivered a particular package. She had no idea, of course—if you wanted to survive the courier business, you never asked the clients their business. As the freak charged into their living room, Fiona plucked a hardcover copy of "Moby Dick" from the nearest bookshelf and hurled it at his skull hard enough to leave a dent; as he writhed on the floor, screeching and muttering, she fetched a long knife from the kitchen and slammed it through his palm, pinning him to the hardwood. In all the excitement, she forgot that Trevor was in the apartment, studying for an organic chemistry exam.

Long story short, Trevor was a little nonplussed to find out her real occupation. And to be fair, maybe she should have trusted him with that information before some Martian crashed into their humble abode, looking for blood. When they broke up, Fiona felt something like relief—no more hiding her true nature from anyone. That's what she loved so much about Bill: not only had he accepted everything about her, but, as the past few weeks had demonstrated, he could deal with any sort of weirdness.

It took them another half-hour to reach the construction site. A high wall of blue-painted plywood marked the perimeter. They walked around it until they reached a chain-link gate on tracks, wide enough to accommodate trucks. On the far side of the gate, beside a gravel roadway leading into the site, stood a double-wide trailer with barred windows and a small wooden porch.

Fiona placed a hand on the edge of the gate, testing its push along the track, when the trailer door opened and a guard sauntered onto the porch. He was portly, with a gray moustache that made him look like a cartoon walrus. Less comical was the pistol dangling from a holster on his hip.

Fiona ducked away from the gate, pulling Bill with her. "What kind of rent-a-cop packs a gun with real bullets?" Bill hissed in her ear.

"One who really doesn't want anyone getting in." As much as Fiona wanted to pull out the phone and search for another hiding spot in the city, a little voice in her head—her personal devil—suggested this situation was worth exploring further. A guard needed a gun to protect something valuable, no?

Bill, her other devil, grinned as he picked up her frequency. "Might as well hide out in a place with our own guard."

"That's right," she said. "It's not like we can get in more trouble than we already are."

How wrong she was.

7

THE DEAN'S NEW LIEUTENANT, Rex, must have possessed some kind of death wish, because he arrived at the Pot O' Gold, the bar that doubled as the Dean's office, in a bright red Ferrari.

It had already been a long afternoon at Long Island City's most legally suspect drinking establishment. In the kitchen, two of the Dean's men scrubbed the tiles with bleach while a third one rolled up a bloody tarp. In the bathroom, a fourth goon used tweezers to pry bits of bone out of the graffiti-scarred wall.

The Dean, atop his usual stool, devoured a steak. Murder always made him hungry, and why not? He was a lion, the unstoppable ruler of this particular veld. Claudius, his bodyguard behind the bar, seemed a little pale after the afternoon's work, and that was okay: sometimes you needed to show these young punks what you were capable of.

He was sawing off a fresh chunk of beef when the gleaming super-car pulled to the curb outside, framed by the front window. When the Dean spied the driver, he slammed his knife into the steak and stood, adjusting the lapels of his suit jacket. Without a word, he extended his hand to Claudius, who retrieved a long steel pipe from its special shelf and placed it gently in the Dean's palm.

Rex entered the bar, the bell over the door ringing merrily. The sight of the Dean, armed, brought him to a startled halt. "Boss?" he asked.

"That," the Dean said, jabbing the pipe at the Ferrari, "is a very ostentatious vehicle."

"Oh, I didn't buy it," Rex said. "I won it at poker."

"Do you know what 'ostentatious' means?" The pipe squeaked as the Dean tightened his grip on it.

Rex locked eyes with Claudius, making a silent plea for help. Claudius shook his head slightly. "I don't," he said, shoulders tensing.

"It means flashy," the Dean said, striding toward him. "It means flamboyant and gaudy. It means something that people notice. It means something that a *cop* might notice, and ask questions, given how it's parked outside a *known criminal establishment*. You get the idea?"

Rex cringed, his hands rising to his face, but the Dean brushed past him and out the door, marching down the sidewalk toward the Ferrari. It was a sunny day, the street dotted with hipsters on the way to lunch at the ridiculously overpriced diner beside the Pot O' Gold. The kids veered wide to avoid him, although it was an open question whether they did so because he held the pipe like a club, or because he had launched into a loud rant about the lack of subtlety in modern culture.

"Better go out there," Claudius told Rex.

"Why?" Rex whined.

"Because otherwise he'll come back inside and crush your skull. It was a long morning."

Rex glanced toward the kitchen, where two men shoved the gore-speckled tarp into a trash bag. "Who was it this time?"

"Pop, finally. Plus his main nurse. Got a little rough." Claudius jutted his chin at the window. "You better get out there. Now."

Rex stepped outside just as the Dean lifted the pipe and brought it down with surgical precision on the left headlight, shattering it. Nodding at the result, the Dean adjusted his grip and smashed the right headlight before moving to the side mirrors. Rex had witnessed his share of rage and destruction, but this was something different: The Dean was cool, methodical, really taking his time and adjusting his angle before every swing.

Across the street, a gaggle of hipsters raised their phones to film the Ferrari's death. The Dean offered them a two-finger salute before driving the pipe into the windshield. The glass splintered around the impact, leaving a hole.

Rex swallowed and shuffled his feet. "You know, I could just…return it?"

"You'll do no such thing, my boy." The Dean swept the pipe along the windshield frame, clearing out the glass. "That's not enough of a lesson here."

"I'm sorry about all this?"

"You phrasing that as an interrogative, as opposed to a declarative, is the rancid cherry atop this particular shit sundae." The Dean drove the pipe into the hood, denting it. "Of course, while failing to keep a low profile is your fault, I am also a little emotional after the action of the past few hours, to put it mildly. Do you realize it's all my firm now?"

Rex, who had no idea what 'interrogative' meant, said: "What can I do to fix this?"

Gritting his teeth, the Dean white-knuckled the pipe.

Instead of swinging away, he forced himself to take a deep breath and set the weapon against the Ferrari. Snapping a handkerchief from his pocket, he wiped his hands. "Fix this? You can't. But if you want to live out the week, you'll help find Bill and Fiona. They're so close I can smell them. Their spoor is failed dreams and all-American grasping."

"Everyone's on it," Rex said, locking eyes with the hipsters across the street, who lowered their phones and slunk away. The Dean could talk all he wanted about "low profile," but his one-man demolition derby might have made him a YouTube star by the end of the day. And what if one of those kids called the police?

A solid whack to the front passenger door separated the panel and sent it clattering to the sidewalk. The Dean paused, his shoulders slumping. "We need to solve Bill and Fiona quickly. Our friend in the north will figure out that we're responsible for his men disappearing, and then we'll have yet another war to wage."

Rex had no idea what the Dean was talking about, but 'our friend in the north' sounded pretty medieval. "And it's delivery day," he said, thinking: maybe I can sell the car parts for scrap. Someone out there could use a supercharged engine, right?

"Yes, yes, yes, and a security change." Tossing the pipe into the gutter, the Dean unscrewed the Ferrari's gas cap. He stuffed his handkerchief partway into the filler pipe. "We're about to make the world's most expensive Molotov cocktail," he announced, patting his pockets.

As he shifted from foot to foot, Rex wondered if a flaming bit of cloth could actually ignite the gas tank. He opened his mouth, closed it, then opened it again. The Dean's search had turned frantic, his hands darting into every pocket of his suit.

Rex's tongue felt too dry and thick. He had to swallow

twice before he could speak. "Sir, I, uh…"

The Dean stopped patting and spun around. His eyes reminded Rex of distant planets seen through a telescope: distant and choked with ice, indifferent to life. "What?"

"What about, um, the low profile?"

The Dean's gaze cracked. Adjusting his lapels, he strode for the bar, his shoes crunching on glass and metal bits on the sidewalk. "You're right, an explosion is a little *gaudy*," he said as he passed Rex. "Just get it out of my sight."

Despite all that damage to the bodywork, the Ferrari started with a magnificent roar when Rex twisted the key. He drove three blocks before remembering the handkerchief still deep in the filler pipe, its end fluttering in the breeze. His foot fluttered on the brake before returning to the gas. Yes, the prospect of spending even another few seconds within a hundred yards of the Dean seemed less appealing than the possibility of exploding into scraps. He shifted into a higher gear and ran the light.

ON THE FAR SIDE OF THE CONSTRUCTION site from the gate, Fiona noticed two boards peeling away from the fence, with enough gap for someone to slip through. Beyond the fence was a field of waist-high weeds, dotted with giant piles of sand. A gray hose snaked around a tall stack of softly rotting lumber, leaking water into a set of bulldozer tracks. Above them rose twenty floors of luxury condo in mid-construction, a maze of concrete and steel frames and wooden planks, the north side plated with windows. The sun glinted off the bright red cage of a construction elevator bolted to an exterior track.

Bill craned his head, using a hand to shield his eyes. "I wonder if that elevator has power."

"We're taking the stairs." Fiona slapped his chest. "It'll be quieter, unless you start panting."

"Don't make fun of my hatred of exercise."

"My turn to take the bag." Fiona eased the sweaty strap off his shoulder and slung it across her chest. The weight of the gold guaranteed her a miserable time up those stairs, but Bill needed a break. His shirt was wet with sweat, his neck red.

Bill kissed her on the forehead and crossed the field toward the condo, weaving around small piles of gravel and rusting rebar. The builders had abandoned this place in a hurry, but not before curtaining the outside of the first floor with orange construction mesh. They pushed through the mesh, into a raw concrete atrium that would someday house an elegant lobby, if work on the place ever started again.

At the far end of the space, beyond the concrete column that encased the empty elevator shaft, they found a stairwell. Bill stepped into the bottom of the well and squinted into the dizzying heights, a puzzle of sunlight and steel extending into infinity. His stomach did a slow somersault.

Placing a hand on his arm, Fiona whispered: "Did you hear something?"

Bill listened, catching the faint rustle of mesh in the wind, a rhythmic clanking that might have been a loose piece of metal somewhere. "Nothing weird."

Fiona drew her pistol. "I'll lead."

They ascended, pausing every other flight to listen. By the tenth floor, Fiona needed to set down the bag and rub her aching shoulder, which was becoming the least of her problems: the cut on her back itched, her ribs throbbed with renewed pain, and her left calf had a nasty twinge that threatened to leave her limping. Her demon laughed at her: You're getting weaker, you loser. You can't. You're not tough enough.

After a few rounds of this mental pummeling, her inner cornerman whispered that a little slowness was okay this week. You survived two car crashes and a couple of beatings, okay? You're human. Now wipe your eyes and get back to it.

As she boxed with her demons, Bill ducked through the fire door. He found a maze of drywall that would someday become apartments, the floors stacked high with marble counters and fixtures draped in dusty plastic. He clicked his tongue until Fiona poked her head through the doorway.

"Remind you of someplace?" Bill asked, throwing his arms wide.

Fiona almost said something sarcastic, before she took another look at the half-completed walls, the angles of the windows, the painted splotches that marked the edges of future rooms. "Actually, yes. Five years ago?"

"Never forget a floorplan, do you?"

"Not when it's part of a job, no." Fiona dropped the bag on a stack of marble. "But this isn't the same place, obviously."

"Maybe the same developer. You know, they're putting up so many of these luxury buildings around here, they probably just use the same plans every time." Bill pointed at the other end of the floor, hidden behind huge bags of plaster and boxes of tools. "Want to see if they have that special something?"

"If they do, might make a good hiding place."

There were no walls or windows on that part of the floor, only a long drop to the weeds below. Bill pointed at the concrete between their feet, dotted and dashed with neon-red paint. "Doesn't seem like they've built it yet, but there are the marks."

"They might have built one on another floor," Fiona said. "Way things are going these days, every rich person wants one."

"Shall we try the penthouse?"

"Might as well. I know you're loving the exercise."

When they reached the top floor (Bill breathing hard through his nose, his feet heavy on the stairs; the bag-strap cutting a fiery line into Fiona's shoulder), the stairs ended in yet another fire door. Fiona pressed an ear to it, listening, before turning the knob and pulling it open a few inches. She paused in the gap.

"We okay?" Bill whispered.

Fiona opened the door wider and stepped through, Bill on her heels. They emerged into a concrete space, empty and featureless except for thick pillars every thirty feet or so. To their left, dusty windows broke the sun into flickering light-ghosts. To their right, the wind rustled across clear plastic sheeting stretched floor to ceiling. Through the plastic: blazing lights, a dark flicker, a flash of blue.

Someone was up here.

Neat as a dance partner, she gripped Bill by the elbow and swept them behind a pillar, hoping nobody on the other side of the plastic saw them silhouetted against the windows. Beneath the wind she heard—or thought she heard—the faint gurgling of water, a footstep.

What the hell was this?

A clank and rumble from the far side of the floor: the construction elevator climbing the building. Maybe headed up here.

You know what this is.

"You have to be kidding me," Bill said, putting the pieces together.

"Leaving now," Fiona replied, ducking low as she scuttled for the door, Bill her shadow. The pillars offered a little bit of cover. Reaching the door, she tried to open it as quietly as possible, wincing as the hinges squeaked. Seven or eight minutes to reach the first floor, she figured, and another couple of minutes to sneak off the lot—

From below came a chorus of footfalls on the stairs.

It sounded like a big crowd.

Headed this way.

They retreated through the door and Fiona had the pistol

leveled as she sought hiding spots, doorways, another stairwell leading down, anything. Somewhere to their right, the unseen elevator screeched to a halt, followed by the metallic slap of its door sliding back. How long until the crowd below reached their level? If there was another set of stairs up here, they could reach the ground that way—

The nearby plastic peeled along a seam, and a man in a white jumpsuit stepped through. A burst of humid air swept through his long black hair. Something about his angular face reminded Fiona of a crow. Beyond his shoulder, as the plastic flapped back into place, Fiona glimpsed what looked like a forest sprouting from the concrete, bathed in the light of a hundred violent suns.

Crow Man regarded them with pale eyes absent of fear or surprise. "You're not the delivery guys," he said.

9

THE PADLOCK KEY OPENED a self-storage unit on the north side of Burlington. Walker flicked on the light before lowering the roll-up door behind him. The bicycle he left outside, propped against a light-pole; it was time to upgrade. The overhead bulbs made the dark green Aston Martin DB Mark III gleam like a sculpture. From the trunk he removed a leather shoulder-bag stuffed with bound stacks of twenty-dollar bills, three full magazines of 9mm ammunition, a pistol and holster, and a phone.

The unit also featured a battered gym locker in the corner, a refugee from the enormous junk-pile beside the storage facility's main gate. Walker opened it to reveal a light gray suit, tailored impeccably to his hundred-seventy pounds. He shed his borrowed two-piece, keeping the shirt, and buttoned himself into his bespoke, instantly feeling more complete. Keeping on his stained socks, he traded his mud-splattered boots for the pair of custom-made leather shoes tucked into the bottom of the locker.

The car offered a reassuring purr, eager to escape the tight confines of the unit. He drove out the main gate of the storage facility, bumping onto the two-lane that would take him to his temporary crash-pad a few miles south. He felt more relaxed with the pistol tucked beneath his armpit, not to mention the bag of cash in the footwell of the passenger seat.

On the console between the seats, his phone rang. He read the number before hitting the speaker button. Asked, in his most relentlessly cheerful voice: "How you doing, Sully?"

"I don't get you, man."

"I didn't realize you had this number."

"This is your old number, man."

"I actually gave it to you? I really am slipping."

"Why'd you run out like that?"

"Aren't you worried the cops are listening to us right now? I mean, since for no reason you think I'm some sort of snitch?"

Sully sighed. "Let's meet up. It's a tense time, you're going through a lot. Happens to all of us. I don't want this to wreck all the history we got together."

"We just chat, have a beer?"

"Exactly."

"Go screw," Walker said, and disconnected the call.

Ten minutes from home he stopped at a gas station. After filling the Aston Martin's tank, he headed inside and bought a jumbo-sized travel mug (in a nuclear shade of orange) along with a small package of instant coffee. The stuff tasted like used motor-oil, in his opinion, but he could use the chemicals for the drive to New York in the morning. "You're welcome, sir," said the kid behind the counter, after ringing up the gas and the purchases.

Walker smiled back. Nothing like a little respect to brighten your day. It made him miss the military, where everyone snapped you a salute when you entered a room. Only he had really screwed that career, hadn't he? That, and everything else in his life.

With a wink, Walker left the kid three twenties in the take-a-penny tray beside the register. Unlocking the car, he scanned the midnight road before climbing in. Beyond the station's island of antiseptic light lay an almost velvety darkness. His lizard brain sensed something out there, despite the lack of movement.

For the rest of the drive, he kept glancing in the rearview mirror every few seconds, and made some extra turns that took him in a long arc through quiet subdivisions.

Home for the moment was a ranch-style house tucked behind a tall hedge, at the end of a cul-de-sac. In the backyard, a creek ran through a deep cut in the earth, fast and rough with summer rainwater. To Walker, it made a nice little moat. The house featured a wraparound front porch, three bedrooms, one and a half baths, a finished basement with racks of tools, a large and gleaming kitchen, a living room with thick carpeting in a spectacularly ugly shade of orange, and a line of bullet-holes in the hallway wall.

In the basement, someone had driven a sledgehammer through the drywall in three spots, dusting the rug white.

In a corner of the master bedroom, a dried brown stain ruined the obnoxious yellow wallpaper.

Yellow crime-scene tape still webbed the back door.

Walker had found the place the previous night, a few hours after crossing the border. Cruising the roads on his new bicycle, he had spied a long piece of yellow tape limp on the gravel driveway, alongside a latex glove wrinkled and pale as a beached jellyfish: signs of a recent cop gathering. The street dark and quiet at that late hour. The front door unlocked.

The crime (whatever its nature) had occurred some time

ago. The blood in the master bedroom was dried to a hard crust, the kitchen counters dusty, the packaged food in the fridge well past its expiration dates. The upstairs closets featured men's and women's clothing, the former in sizes too small for his needs. Under different circumstances, Walker might have felt the faint sadness that sometimes comes when standing in an abandoned space. But the prospect of hot running water and a real mattress overrode any melancholy.

Now, having dodged Sully and retrieved his property, it was time at last for a good scrubbing. After parking the Aston Martin in the backyard, he went inside and locked the doors and drew a bath, placing the phone and pistol on the tile beside the tub. He preferred showers, but feared the hiss of falling water would disguise a breaking window, a furtive step on the stairway.

Before bed, Walker took two thin-stemmed wine-glasses from the kitchen and two hardcover books from the shelf in the living room and propped the books against the front and back doors with a glass balanced atop each. From the recycling bin underneath the sink he fished an armful of empty tin cans and walked through the house placing them on the closed windows, beside the locks. He even did the ones in the basement, barely large enough for a child to crawl through.

He kept the door of the master bedroom open, to better hear any glass breaking or tin toppling, and lay in the tub after padding its bottom with a pair of thick blankets. He placed the pistol on the tile again, within easy reach.

He had always slept lightly. Any sound could snap him from the deepest dreams.

The night stayed silent.

In the gray hour before dawn he opened his eyes and believed for a freezing second that his daughter was sitting on the toilet with a rifle, watching him, until he blinked and her familiar face dissolved into the play of light and shadow on the bathroom wall. He climbed out of the tub, shaking the blood back into his knees and hands, just as glass shattered downstairs.

Walker slipped on his shoes and suit in record time. Chambered a pistol round as he left the bedroom. The upstairs hallway hazy with smoke. He crouched at the head of the stairs, weapon aimed at the sliver of front door visible through the banisters. The polished floorboards at the foot of the stairs flickered orange with reflected flame.

A window broke in the living room, the tin can toppling from its perch beside the lock. A wine bottle rolled toward the kitchen doorway, trailing a stream of orange flame. Sully must have found him somehow. He had taken care to cover his tracks, but Burlington is a small place.

Walker crept to the ground floor, heat baking his skin, coughing on the gray smoke clouding the light. The top half of the front door was pebbled glass with clear edges. Keeping low, he peeked through the bottom rim and saw one of Sully's men standing next to a black pickup truck parked in the driveway, dressed in a black windbreaker and a bullet-resistant vest, a lit Molotov cocktail in his hand.

Walker turned and scrambled for the rear of the house. The kitchen was already ablaze. The back door cracked open, framing Sully's second bodyguard behind the Aston Martin. The man had a rifle cradled in his arms, his expression patient as a deer hunter in a blind.

The front-door window shattered, along with the bottle hurled through it. The curtains framing the door dissolved in flame, the paint bubbling and peeling. Walker's body kicked into emergency mode, sweat soaking his shirt and suit, his hands slippery on the gun. He opened the door that led to the basement. Fast down the stairs. Smoke seeping through the cracks in the ceiling, like gray fingers reaching for him.

Too late he remembered the shoulder-bag still in the upstairs bedroom, with the money in it. At least he had his wallet and keys and phone in his pants pockets.

Jamming the pistol into his waistband, he threw the latch on one of the small windows that opened onto the crawl-space beneath the porch, slamming it open with the heel of his hand. Stuck an arm through the gap and tried to slither through. His body jammed at the shoulder. Smoke raked his nostrils, trickling his throat. No good, man. You're trapped.

He relaxed and let his body drop back into the basement. Fumbled through the nearest rack of tools for anything that might help, his shaking fingers spilling coffee cans full of nails and screws on the floor. Warm metal slapped his fore-arm. A pry-bar on a hook. Yes.

He swung the bar at the window-frame, the bent claw biting into the wood, and pulled as hard as he could. The house dying around him, crackling and roaring as flame filled its rooms. A smoke detector shrieked once and fell silent. He braced a foot against the basement wall and strained on the bar, regretting every missed gym session and extra glass of whiskey.

The window-frame tore free of the wall, spraying him with glass and wood. Walker dropped the pry-bar and hoisted himself through the rough opening, wide enough this time for his shoulders to fit through, his suit tearing on the brick. Wriggling for daylight, his back scraping the underside of the porch, the pistol held in front of him.

Wooden latticework sealed off the crawl-space from the lawn. Through its diamond-shaped holes, Walker spied Sully's man still beside the truck, gaze focused on the sec-ond-story windows. Walker aimed the pistol and fired four times, the bodyguard collapsing as bullets bit into his legs.

The fifth shot went through the top of his head.

When the other man rounded the corner of the house, Walker shot him in the ankle and, as he fell, the neck. After shoving his way through the latticework, he ransacked the bodies for anything of use, which came to eighty-three dollars, another phone, and a rifle and pistol. Straining to hear sirens over the crackle of burning wood, he jogged for the backyard, bracing himself for the worst. Nobody had touched the Aston Martin, thankfully.

As Walker accelerated out of the backyard and down the driveway, flames punched out the first-floor windows: red hands waving him a cheerful goodbye. He felt jubilant, like he always did after firefights. Nothing like dodging bullets to make you feel more alive.

For added laughs, he dialed Sully, waiting until the highway sign welcoming him to the great state of New York disappeared in his rearview mirror.

"You're dead," Sully said.

"You know, for a guy who grows weed and talks a lot of I Ching bullshit about rolling with the punches, you sure don't stay relaxed when things don't go your way."

Sully laughed like a buzzsaw choking on a thick piece of wood. "You think I won't find you? You know how easy it was to find you before?"

"How'd you do it?"

"Like I'd tell you. You're real lucky you left me with a mess to clean up here. It'll take a little time before I can focus on you. But don't you fret, I'm coming for your ass real soon."

"I guess the friendship is over, huh?" Walker said.

Before Sully could reply, Walker disconnected the call. His mirth had cooled, leaving him with a roiling gut. His hands stank of smoke.

10

FIONA AIMED HER PISTOL between Crow Man's eyes. "That's right," she said. "We're not the delivery folks."

Ninety-nine times out of a hundred, pointing a weapon in someone's face made them flinch. Crow Man was a very special case. He smiled and nodded, biting his lower lip, as if Fiona had presented him with a tantalizing dessert. "Inevitable," he said. "I told him this would happen."

"Bill," Fiona said through gritted teeth, "will you please check this gentleman for weapons?"

"I'm not armed," Crow Man said, as Bill circled toward him. "Well, armed in the sense that I have arms, with hands and fingers and all that, but I don't have any weapons. I'm a pacifist. Too many guns in the world."

"Don't disagree with you there, buddy," Fiona said, stepping closer. "But raise your arms—your real arms, with the fingers on the end—so we can get on with this."

While Crow Man followed orders, Bill dropped his duffel bag on the concrete, stooped, and patted down the man's ankles, thighs, waist, shoulders, feeling nothing but taut muscle under the jumpsuit. The guy stank of weed. Or maybe that was the smell wafting through the split plastic behind them.

"He's clean," Bill said, stepping away to retrieve his bag.

"I'm guilty, is what I am." Arms still raised, Crow Man locked gazes with Bill. "Ever wonder if today is your last day?"

"Only every morning." With a grunt, Bill lifted the bag onto his shoulder, which felt raw after their cross-borough run. Maybe a puff or two of this strange dude's weed would sort him out, after they reached some kind of safety.

Fiona heard the footsteps in the stairwell, louder, hammering, like the sound of her doom rushing down. Or maybe it was her heart slamming against her ribs. "Spare me the existential navel-gazing," she said, waving her pistol at the shimmering lab behind him. "Let's go in there."

"The grand tour," Crow Man said, leading them through the plastic sheeting. "I'm the chief horticulturalist of this particular institution. Also the chemist."

Fiona counted twenty, twenty-five, thirty long rows of marijuana in huge pots, the stems held upright by twine webs, bathed by hot lights overhead. Between the lights, silver ventilation tubes hummed. Across a narrow aisle from the plants, on wooden tables that ran the length of the floor, she saw cardboard boxes piled high with plastic bags full of weed; and below the tables, plastic drums and tool boxes on rolling pallets.

"Biggest bloom room I've ever seen," Bill muttered.

"Thank you," Crow Man said. "If you want to sample anything, feel free. I'm always in a hospitable mood when someone has a pistol to my head."

Over the thump of machinery and the hiss of mechanical

air, Fiona caught faint voices. The people from the elevator. Crap. "Tell me who they are," she said.

Crow Man shrugged. "The real delivery people, probably."

"And who's on the stairs?" Bill asked.

"New security." Crow Man tapped his temple. "Wrong hour for you to show up. Shift change and delivery? Glory, glory, glory, paranoia."

Fiona directed them into the nearest row, the plants tall enough to hide them if they crouched a bit. "Whose place is this?"

"Rockaway," Crow Man said. "New venture, big money."

Bill giggled. It was an ugly sound, muffled by the knuckle in his mouth. Fiona punched him in the shoulder, her usual move when he did something antisocial, but her own lips were pulling back, her throat hitching with laughter.

Crow Man's face twitched with confusion.

"The Good Lord himself," Bill informed him, "has taken a personal interest in screwing up our lives."

"We're overdue for payback," Fiona added. "Too much killing. Too much bullshit. Too many parking tickets."

Beyond the plastic sheeting, the door clanged open, followed by the rapid drumbeat of boots. Someone yelled a greeting.

"Anyway, we need your panic room," Bill hissed in Crow Man's ear.

"There's a lot of panic in here," Crow Man agreed, nodding.

"Where is it?" Wrapping a hand around the back of Crow Man's neck, Bill squeezed hard.

"Safe room, separate room, locked room," Fiona murmured, scrambling for synonyms as she adjusted her sweaty grip on the pistol.

Crow Man's eyes widened, and he jabbed a finger to their

left. "Oh, yes. The most special room. My place of worship. Down there."

Bill followed that finger through shifting leaves, spying a flash of metal. No way to see more from this angle. He wondered if it was really a door. If the panic room had a working lock and finished walls. Add to that Crow Man's mention of "place of worship," and Bill had no doubt that some spectacular weirdness awaited them in there. But it's not like we have a choice. Either we go for it, or these men kill us.

"No time like the present," Fiona said, and stood, her pistol dug into Crow Man's neck hard enough to make him wince.

As she shuffled her hostage into the aisle, a half-dozen men appeared at the far end: big muscles, bad tattoos, shaved heads, body armor. High-priced merc security, the kind that Rockaway hired for top dollar, but nobody she recognized. At least she wouldn't have to kill anyone she knew, if it came to that. She was tired of murdering folks, whether or not they deserved death.

The men yelled in unison and reached for their weapons. Fiona twisted her body behind Crow Man, trying to give them as small a target as possible, and tugged on his collar. Crow Man took a hesitant step backward, then another.

Bill stepped behind Fiona, hoping that Crow Man provided enough cover for the two of them—and at that most excellent moment, he heard a faint sound that sent an iron spike of pure terror through his heart: the faint purr of fabric ripping. The gold clanked as it shifted, and he glanced down as the bottom of the bag split open an inch.

Fiona bumped into him. "Better move," she hissed through her teeth.

"Bag's ripping," Bill said, trying to adjust his grip so his hand covered the growing hole.

Fiona pushed into him again, harder, as he looped his arms around the bag, cradling it like a baby. That would hold for a few more minutes or until their gruesome deaths, whichever came first.

Bill retreated for the panic room, Fiona almost on top of him, Crow Man shuffling with his hands up. The stark light twisted and lengthened their shadows into a monstrous centipede.

"This will go better if you stop," said one of the mercs, cocking his head. They were too close, a few of them drifting into the weed aisles.

Fiona snorted loduly over the hum of equipment.

Bill's fingers ached, the gold digging into his palms. The bag was still coming apart, strand by strand, but the door to the panic room was only a few feet away, close enough to see that it lacked knobs or keyholes. Hopefully it'll open if I push, Bill thought. If it doesn't, we're pinned.

"Good day to die," Crow Man said, loud and cheerful.

They reached the door. Sweating, half-expecting a bullet to crash into his chest, Bill pressed a hand against the cold steel and pushed. It refused to budge, and his stomach flipped. Was it locked?

He shoved harder, and the door hummed open, on springs, revealing a room lit pale by fluorescent tubes. Stacks of cardboard boxes lined the steel walls, along with shrink-wrapped bales of cash. He stepped inside and saw a giant red button beside the door, with the words 'PRESS TO LOCK' on the wall above it in big red type.

In the doorway, Fiona planted a hard boot in Crow Man's back, sending him sprawling into the aisle. She ducked into the panic room, and Bill hit the button. The door wheezed shut, blocking the sight of more men charging through the weed forest. With a roar of relief, Bill dropped the ruined duffel bag on the floor, and it tore open, scattering rough gold chunks across the featureless concrete floor.

The door's heavy bolts slammed home. Fiona looked at Bill, jabbed a thumb at the cash. "How much you think is in here?"

"Enough to buy a small country," Bill said.

"If only we could see the Dean's face when he hears about this. His head will explode." Chuckling, Fiona pulled out her phone. No signal. The universe obviously wanted them to play this game on the Nightmare Difficulty setting.

Leaning against the wall, forcing herself to take measured breaths, Fiona cycled through her memory. Had she seen a keypad outside the door? She didn't think so. Maybe this model only locked when someone inside hit that button. The big dudes outside could take a cutting torch to the door, or explosives, but it might take hours for them to get in here. Maybe days, if they were lucky.

"Gonna take inventory," she said.

"If there's some aspirin," Bill said, wincing as he rotated his shoulder, "I could use, like, ten. Along with a big shot of vodka."

"You and me both, love." She started at the far end of the room, where three small propane tanks sat on a rolling pallet, alongside four full water-cooler jugs, but no stove or water-cooler. The pallet pinned a single-gear bicycle with a heavy red frame to the wall. The bicycle had a fat pair of training wheels bolted to its rear frame.

Fiona opened a long metal box beside the door and found two fire extinguishers, a box of flares, a fire-retardant blanket, duct tape, two gas masks, and a small medical kit. So at least they had some safety supplies, but what she really wanted for Christmas was a metric shit-ton of ammunition. What kind of self-respecting drug lab didn't have an armory of some sort?

At least the medical kit had ibuprofen in little packets. She dry-swallowed five pills before tossing three packets to Bill, who was standing in the center of the space, pointing at the ceiling. "There's a vent," he said. "Too small to crawl through, though, unless I lost, like, a hundred and forty pounds."

"There's also a tragic lack of secret hatches in the floor," Fiona replied, stomping on the concrete before resuming her search. Another metal box, in the opposite corner, looked enticingly like a gun locker. Opening it shattered her hopes: instead of weapons, she found a plastic doll of a woman, nude and life-size and disturbingly pink.

"I wouldn't touch that," Bill said. "Not unless you want a juicy case of syphilis."

"I can scrub my skin with bleach," Fiona said, slamming the lid shut. "But there's no bleach that can clean the memory of that from my head."

"Hey, check this out." Bill tilted an open cardboard box so she could see a collection of wigs, fake jewelry, and women's clothing. Using two fingers, he pulled up the leg of a light blue pantsuit. "What's he doing, dressing it up like Hillary Clinton?"

"I like to think I'm open about folks' sex lives. Live and let live," Fiona said. "But then I see something like this, and I'm all like, 'Kill it with fire.'"

"When I was a kid, we broke into this old dude's house down the road, found a sex doll in the garage," Bill giggled. "The sick bastard had put a rubber Ronald Reagan mask over the head. It was a female doll, by the way."

"Who didn't want to bang the Gipper?" Wiping her hands on her jeans, Fiona shifted to the boxes beside the doll locker, which held more energy bars in weirder flavors (she dared not taste *Pink-Bubble-Crunch!*) along with neon-colored energy drinks. In the last box, she found cardboard cartons with black cobras winding above militaristic script: fireworks.

"Because when I'm running a top-secret drug lab," Bill said, when she held up a box, "I like to unwind after a long day by shooting off loud, colorful fireworks on top of a building that everyone can see for miles around. That's not conspicuous at all."

No ammunition! Anger roared through Fiona, hot and electric, and she kicked a stack of boxes away from the wall beside the door—revealing an intercom with three buttons and a small screen embedded above a speaker.

At least this was something she could use. Pressing the red button made the screen snap to life, revealing a line of men standing in front of the door, pistols and rifles raised as if they expected Bill and Fiona to merrily waltz out. Idiots. Based on the angle, the camera was embedded in the top of the doorway.

Bill peeled open the energy bar. "Want to hear the good news?" he asked.

Taking a seat on a million dollars in twenties, Fiona popped the magazine from her pistol and did a shell count, shucking the brass into her lap: a ritual that always soothed her. "Sure."

"We wanted a secure place to lie low." Bill took a bite, chewing hard, and spread his arms wide. "Hey, mission accomplished."

11

TWO HUNDRED MILES from Brooklyn, Walker made a point of keeping under the speed limit, praying that no cop would pull him over to admire the car. His identification would check out, but the ripped suit and the smell of smoke might raise some questions. The pistol was tucked under the driver's seat, the rifle stashed in the trunk, and Walker had no intention of causing trouble until he crossed the East River.

In New Jersey, he noted more police presence: helicopters overhead, cruisers howling down the left lane every few minutes. Raindrops spattered the windshield, blurring the slowing traffic. An electronic road sign flashed dire warnings about weather and delays. Trapped behind a truck, Walker sighed and flicked on the radio. The newscaster babbled about explosive vests and fundamentalism. A guest interrupted to wonder if the country was in trouble. When is the country not in trouble, Walker almost shouted back.

The storm passed as soon as he crossed the Brooklyn Bridge. Entering the borough of his birth felt as warm and welcoming as slipping back into that bespoke suit after all his time up north. The stately apartment buildings shaded with a couple decades' worth of car exhaust and industrial soot, the dingy pagodas with barred windows, the hip eateries where bright white light reflected off blonde wood—he loved every inch of it. The sight of a crushed beer-can on the rain-slick sidewalk brought back memories of his teenage years in Bushwick, and the summer parties where he would crouch in a cool corner with a moisture-beaded bottle of beer, listening to tattooed gargoyles discuss the finer points of music and heroin: his years before the military, and all the messiness after.

When Walker turned onto Metropolitan Avenue and Driggs, he opened the glove compartment and removed a slim plastic fob, pressed a button. Down the block, at the base of a steel building as angular as a knife, a garage door rose. He maneuvered into a concrete cube lined with other luxury vehicles, backing into his designated space with inches to spare on either side. The Aston Martin was not a vehicle you parked on the street, no matter how gentrified this neighborhood had become in the past decade.

An elevator took him to the third floor, where he unlocked the blank metal door that led to his condo. After throwing the four deadbolts, he shed his shoes on a small rug in the entranceway and padded into his place for the first time in many months.

The interior of his apartment was a spread from an upscale furniture catalogue, spare and pale, with some whimsical touches. The Buddha in the living room, smiling from a deep shelf built into the wall. The framed, yellowing Wanted poster for John Dillinger in the hallway leading to the bathroom. Walker liked to think this place had the most character of any unit in the building, although he knew that particular bar was not hard to clear. His neighbors on all sides were finance bros, the kind who decorated mostly with empty bottles of vodka and pizza boxes.

Every surface had a fine coating of dust. Walker never employed a cleaning service. It would take an hour to wipe everything down, once he completed some pressing tasks. He peeled off his ruined suit and folded it neatly before depositing it, with a sigh, atop a pile of faded and torn clothing in the hallway closet. It always hurt to lose a good two-piece, although he had seven more in the bedroom.

After disposing of his ripped ensemble, he showered and dressed in a pair of designer jeans and a plain white t-shirt before heading into the kitchen, where he ground a few ounces of the ultra-caffeinated coffee he liked.

While he waited for the coffee to steep in the French press, he walked into the tiny office off the kitchen and spun the dial on the Döttling faux-antique safe beside the desk. The heavy door opened to reveal a wood-lined tray honeycombed with five circular holes, each filled with an expensive watch that glittered under the safe's dim light. The deep drawer beneath the tray held a few stacks of cash, three passports, a handful of phones, and an old (and much beloved) pair of brass knuckles.

Back in the living room, he sank into the oversized leather chair beside the window, sipping his giant mug of coffee. Despite the shower, he could still smell the smoke on his skin. He made a phone call. The man on the other side suggested meeting at Walker's favorite bar, which was no surprise.

With an hour to burn, he flicked on the television. More death and destruction, on every channel. He raised the remote, about to turn it off, when the image cut to a Tesla parked in Union Square, its windshield spattered red, a pixelated mess hanging out the open driver's window. An unusual murder in Manhattan, a voice droned. Another cut, to a familiar mugshot of the prime suspect, handsome and heavy-jawed.

Walker settled back in his chair, smiling. That was Fiona's boyfriend for you: too flashy for his own good, without much to back it up. At least that confirmed his earlier guess, that the two of them had headed back to New York. You still got your hunting instincts, old man.

It also ratcheted up the urgency of his mission. Fifty minutes later, he headed four blocks east—and found his favorite bar erased.

How many nights had he spent at a back table in that pleasant stinkhole, smoking small Cuban cigars in defiance of the city's health laws, as he downed pint after pint? But during his time in Canada, someone had purchased the Dog and *gentrified* it into a monstrosity.

The new owners had painted the walls sky-blue and hung velvet paintings of bulldogs every few feet. They had replaced the tables with long picnic tables designed to foster love and community. The speakers overhead blared a pop song that sounded like a castrato trapped in a video arcade.

As he ordered a microbrew at the bar, Walker felt like he was attending a wake for someone that nobody in the room had liked. Bearded kids kept their heads down, dour and silent as they tapped away at their phones. He remembered how, in the nights following the collapse of the Twin Towers, people had crowded the bars, went home with strangers, knocked on their neighbors' doors for the first time: anxious for any sort of connection, to feel united with the living. Most of the people in this bar had been small children at the turn of the century, and grew up with the omnipresent fear of the hijacked airplane, the backpack stuffed with explosives left under a bus seat. They were too frightened by existence to do anything other than stare at little screens.

His contact, sitting at the picnic table closest to the rear wall, blended into these fancy environs as well as a hyena in a nursery. The cheery lights glinted off the man's bald head, well-hatched with deep scars. The music seemed to ratchet something in his body inch by painful inch, his hands gripping his full pint glass harder and harder.

"Dash. Long time no see," Walker said, taking a seat where he could see the bar and front door. Two old warriors perched beside one another, drawing anxious side-glances from the kids.

Dash's eyes widened in fake surprise. "I'm amazed, man," he said. "I've never seen a ghost before."

Walker shrugged. "Told you I retired."

"Yes, you did," Dash said. "But you wouldn't believe the rumors. For months everybody was convinced someone had finally double-tapped you, tossed the body in the water. When you didn't wash up, they said someone pulled a Jimmy Hoffa, buried you in a foundation somewhere."

"People love to chat, don't they?"

"Anyway, so now you're back." Dash flashed his teeth. "And I bet it's because of your dear daughter."

Walker shrugged. "She's been a busy girl."

"You approve of her lifestyle?"

"No, but she's going to do what she wants. At least she's really good at what she does, even if it isn't very nice."

"Well, she's been doing unkind things for a pretty nasty crew. We're talking the sort of guys who'd sell their mothers into sexual slavery for a buck ninety-five."

"Charming." Walker leaned close. "You'll watch how you talk about my kid."

Dash raised his hands, palms out. "No offense. I know

what it's like, not being around a lot for my daughter. I feel guilty, too."

"Now you're just poking me."

"Can't resist. You're too serious."

"I know I could've been around more for her," Walker said, refusing to let it go. "But I had a job to do. As did you. I've tried to have a normal relationship with her. I'm still trying. Don't mention it again, or I'll tell people that you're speaking to me. That's a potential career-ender for you."

Dash winked. "Or a career-maker."

Walker took a sip of beer. "Color me intrigued."

"Things haven't changed since you were shooting folks in the head for Uncle Sam. The FBI is almost totally focused on stopping terrorism. We're also tasked with pushing back against the cartels, along with our good friends at the DEA. Which doesn't leave a lot of budget or manpower for anything else."

"That's why you pay contractors like me."

"And quite handsomely, I might add. You made what, a thousand dollars a day in Iraq?"

"Hazard pay," Walker said, neglecting to mention the real payday that had taken place in Baghdad, near the end of his last contract. Some off-the-books work with a few trusted friends, working off a tip yanked out of a former Republican Guard colonel (along with most of the man's teeth). Why deal with red tape and taxes when you can walk away with millions of Saddam's bunker dollars?

"More than I've ever seen in my paycheck. I should have gone freelance, instead of carrying a badge." Dash leaned back. "The guys your daughter works for, the Rockaway Mob, they're small fry compared to the other groups on our list, but they're a rough crew. Twenty, thirty years ago, we'd have a task force dedicated to bringing them down. These days, we can't spare the agents."

"I get the idea," Walker said. "And I think I know where you're going with this."

"Let's say—speaking hypothetically—that a real hero destroyed the Rockaway Mob. Dismantled their operations, made their people disappear for good. If something like that occurred, the FBI would certainly owe that person a big favor."

"Speaking hypothetically, what kind of favor?"

"In this hypothetical world, there's only so much the FBI could do on a local level. That being said, I think the FBI could persuade the NYPD and the DA to stop caring about the hero's daughter. I imagine they'd appreciate the Rockaway Mob going bye-bye. It's in their backyard, after all."

"What about the daughter's loser boyfriend?"

"Are we talking about dropping all charges for him, or making sure nobody finds the body?"

Walker made a three-act play of puzzling it over. "Dropping all charges, I guess. Unless he opens his smart mouth at the wrong moment."

"I'm sure something could be arranged."

"Whatever the deal, this hero would need it in writing. Signed, sealed, delivered."

"We might not have time for lawyers." Dash checked his watch, a battered warhorse that Walker remembered from their days in the field together. "But you have my word—and you know my word is good—that we'll work this out for you. The question is, are we good?"

Walker downed his beer. "We're good. You have eyes on my kid?"

"Queens, last I heard, which was a couple hours ago. This new system we have, facial recognition and geolocation, ultra-fast, it's really something to see. Rang cherries on some security-cam footage, she and her boyfriend running across a street. Since then, nothing." Dash slapped the table and stood to leave. "I'll email the intel I got. Same address?"

"Yeah." Walker stood.

"You good on equipment? I have a connection, lend you some heavy-gauge stuff."

Walker thought about the foldaway panel in the rear of his closet, and the things in the hideaway behind it. "I always bring my own tools."

Dash grinned. "I'd expect nothing less."

Walker drained his beer, offered Dash a quick salute, and marched for the exit. The lighting, the music, the hipsters seemed to grate on him more with each passing step. By the time he reached the door, his jaw was clenched tight, his hands in loose fists. It took every ounce of his considerable self-control to not slam a boot through the door, or snatch a random glass off the bar and send it through the window with its idiotic puppy stencil.

Back on the street, he filled his lungs with cool night air and held it. The rage had nothing to do with those angel-headed hipsters, of course. It was all about Fiona. He was going to take all that rage and use it to rip apart everyone threatening her. And if Bill didn't survive—well, Walker always told Fiona that she should trade up.

His phone rang.

12

A BIG BLACK CAR ANGLED for the gleaming bull's eye of the Holland Tunnel. In the front passenger seat, Sully took an epic hit of his most powerful weed before passing the joint to his three men squeezed in the back. The driver squinted through the smoggy windshield, unfamiliar with the terrain. It was a big risk, smoking up as they neared one of the most-surveilled places on the East Coast, but Sully liked how the danger amped him up.

Besides, if a cop pulled them over, the weed might end up the least of their problems. In the trunk, nestled beneath a geologic layer of dirty clothes, Sully had tucked five automatic rifles—one for each man in the car. It was a lot of firepower for a straightforward job, but Sully believed that, when it came to Walker, overkill was a virtue.

13

THE CONSTRUCTION ELEVATOR was little more than a cage with a control box and a sliding door. As it ascended, the wind whistled through its steel grating, a mournful sound interrupted every few seconds by the Dean cracking his knuckles. The popping bones made the men around him twitch as one. Through the grating, they had a sweeping view of the Queens waterfront, the glass skyscrapers glittering in the dusk.

It never ends, the Dean mused. You can kill your rivals. You can kill your business partners. You can kill your head of security. But the problems never stop cropping up, because criminality attracts morons who literally can't function in normal society. Which makes it similar to academia, when you really think about it. Why did I bother leaving the university?

The Dean turned to Rex and asked: "What else was in there?"

"Some money," Rex muttered.

The Dean balled his hands into fists. "I need grand totals, boy. It was delivery day, after all."

Rex swallowed hard. "Five million, I think?"

The men behind the Dean stepped back until their spines flattened against the grating. They were hulking as football players, and tough, but none wanted to deal with the Dean throwing fists in an enclosed space. They considered their take-home pay generous enough to deal with their employer's eccentricities.

But this time, the Dean surprised them. Instead of trying to slam Rex's head into the wall, he closed his eyes and rotated his neck until the joint popped. "Seems high," he said, so quietly it was almost lost in the grinding of the elevator's gears.

"Our friends up north paid some tribute. We were using this place as the waypoint. Figured it'd be okay with the added security."

"Yes, if any of you knuckle-draggers were halfway competent," the Dean said. "Honestly, this all comes down to killing two people. Is that really too much to ask?"

Before anyone could reply, the elevator thumped to a halt, and the door rattled back to reveal pure chaos. Someone had torn down part of the plastic wall that shielded the weed forest from the elements, the precious plants rustling in the high-altitude breeze. Mercs in body armor stood among the rows of plants, their pistols aimed at the steel door of the panic room.

As the Dean strode into the forest, Crow Man scuttled beside him. "Thank you for swinging by," he said, as if the Dean was there for a quick drink and a chat.

The Dean had no use for small talk. Jutting his chin at the steel door, he said: "Is there a keypad?"

"No. Just one button, on the inside. Doesn't lock unless you hit it. They hit it." Crow Man punched air as he danced from foot to foot, clearly agitated.

The Dean pointed at the tables to their left, and the tool boxes beneath. "How long to cut through it? I trust you have something suitable down there?"

Crow Man snorted laughter. "It's two feet of steel. You got a nuke in your back pocket?"

"An answer, please."

Crow Man punched air again. "I don't know, a day or two? If they don't shoot back, or try anything tricky?"

They arrived at the door, and the Dean craned his head, examining the seamless steel. "Can we cut off their oxygen?"

"Again, I don't know. I think there's a vent somewhere." Crow Man waved a finger at the ceiling. "Like, on the roof. But what if we cut off their air, and they don't come out? It's not just the money in there. They got my favorite toys, too."

The Dean shuddered to think what might serve as the favorite toys of Crow Man, who once snorted so much bad meth he tried to build a time machine from a tape recorder and a car battery. The guy might have been a stellar chemist and a better botanist, but sane he was not.

"Then we can cut through it at our leisure." The Dean sneered at the door. "When last I checked, I owned this building."

"We got a time limit on that money, chief," Crow Man said. "Folks expecting delivery real soon."

"Ah, yes. Right." The Dean cracked his knuckles again. "Any way to communicate in?"

Crow Man nodded. "They have an intercom. It's got a camera, too."

A soft click, barely audible over the gurgle of the ventilation system, followed by a thunderous voice: *"Is that my good buddy?"*

The Dean startled. "Bill?"

"*It is!*" Biblical Bill boomed from a speaker in the ceiling. "*Hey, honey, look at the screen! It's that dimwit who used to pay us!*"

The Dean, his cheeks reddening, ran his hands over the doorframe until he found the black dot of a miniature camera lens. "Come out of there, you little shit," he hissed into it. "Or we'll only make it that much more unpleasant when we get inside."

"*Um, let me think about that.*" A click, and a long pause.

The Dean froze.

Another click. "*After a lengthy period of careful deliberation, we've decided to decline your offer. Fuck off and die.*"

The Dean stepped back, struggling against the smile tugging the edges of his lips. Despite his rage, he felt almost giddy. When was the last time he'd faced an interesting opponent?

"Dear boy," the Dean said, removing his suit jacket and draping it carefully on the nearest table. "We find ourselves at a bit of an impasse here. The unstoppable force—that's me—has encountered an immovable object. That's the room you're in."

Click. "*Wait, let me guess: you're going to try and bore us out of here.*"

"Oh, it's going to be more kinetic than that, don't worry." The Dean rolled up his sleeves. "By the way, a hearty hello to Fiona. We have unfinished business, dear."

"*That's right,*" Fiona laughed. "*My boot hasn't finished up your ass yet.*"

The Dean's memories drifted to destroying the Ferrari that afternoon. How its sleek metal had crumpled as easily as paper under his confident blows. It was a real thrill, ruining something beautiful. Like Fiona's face.

"*Near as I can count,*" Fiona continued, "*there's maybe*

four million dollars in here." The amplified sound of shredding, loud as a fender-bender. *"Whoops, there goes a hundred bucks. How much of this can we rip up before you get in here?"*

From his hip pocket, the Dean drew a small tan bag, made of wrinkled material. He shook it, and something jangled inside. It sounded like coins. "Bill," he said. "You remember Pop, correct? Such a terrifying individual, his bedridden state didn't stop people from shitting themselves in his presence. You could say he had real big balls."

Crow Man cocked an eyebrow, as if to say: This is too crazy, even for me.

The Dean shook his change purse. "Turns out, his balls weren't all that impressive. I can barely fit three quarters in here." Returning it to his pocket, he shot his cuffs and smiled.

"If you do try to get in," Fiona added, *"there's a couple of propane tanks in the corner here. We might die, but we'll make a real bonfire on our way out, understand?"*

"Perfectly." The Dean spun on his heel and paced down the nearest marijuana row, the leaves brushing his shoulders. The merc in his path stepped aside, and the Dean paused. Something clipped to the man's vest interested him a good deal. In fact, it presented an elegant solution to this siege.

14

WATCHING THE DEAN PACE on the tiny video screen, Bill offered a hearty thumbs-up. "As much as I hate this guy, he did the world a favor by taking out Pop. That dude always freaked me out. Not to the point where I shit myself, I hasten to add."

Fiona tore open an energy bar and wolfed it down. It tasted like crap, but she wanted the calories and sugar. As her adrenaline faded, her pains returned with fangs. Her back muscles twinged around the staples, her bruises throbbed, and her left eyelid had decided this was the perfect time to start twitching. "What are they doing?"

"The Dean's lecturing everyone, as usual." Bill wiped the sweat from his forehead. "It's getting hotter. Is there a fan or something in here?"

"Probably not installed yet," Fiona said, waving her hand below the ceiling vent. "You want some water?"

"I'm okay." Stacking two bundles of money into a soft stool, Bill sat with his back against the wall. "Want a quickie?"

Fiona grinned. "Maybe when we're not surrounded by an

army of gunmen."

"Oh, come on. You mean the prospect of being shot to death isn't a turn-on?"

Digging into the box beside her, Fiona held up two more energy bars. "You want chocolate or vanilla? Better get some food in you. Could be a long night."

"Chocolate." He tore the wrapping off the bar and chewed. It tasted like flavored drywall, but better than nothing. He pined for a shot of espresso, and maybe a shortbread cookie to go with it. Heck, why not fantasize about sitting outside a Barcelona cafe, watching the crowds walk through the heat and sunlight?

"Can I ask you something? It's something that's been in my head for weeks, but I haven't…"

Fiona rolled her eyes. "Spit it out, sweetie. No time like the present."

Bill took his time chewing the last of his energy bar. "If we make it out of here, what are we going to do? We can't run forever."

"Our retirement plans hinge entirely on neutralizing every fucker out there," Fiona said. "If we figure that out, we can do anything we want. Where do you want to go?"

"Spain?"

"Sure." Fiona slapped a stack of money. "With this sort of cash, we'd live like royalty."

"Where you want to live?"

"Montreal, maybe. I went there once, for work, remember? Cool place. We could learn French, pretend we're hipsters, listen to Leonard Cohen in bars."

"Too cold in the winter."

Fiona smiled. "The tropics didn't work out too well for us."

"My big lesson from that: No matter what, we gotta stick

together. My brains, your brawn." Bill held up his hands, palms out, as if she might smack him. "Just kidding. You know I can take care of myself. Everything that's happened to us over the past couple days? I think I'm getting more of a taste for the rough stuff."

"Well, don't get too used to it. I'm trying to cut back. Wherever we go next, I don't want to hurt people anymore, okay?" Fiona lifted her pistol and ejected the magazine. "I'm forever done with this bullet shit. It's blades to ploughshares."

"If we don't kill anything other than beers for the rest of our natural lives, I'm fine with that," Bill said. "Whatever works. I love you."

"I love you, too." She snapped home the magazine. "The only moment I ever wavered, it was in Oklahoma, when I wondered if you'd actually dumped me. That night I caught up with you, I was angry as hell."

"When I left New York, I was worried that if you knew anything, if I'd told you anything, that the Dean would have killed you to get to me."

"And you were probably right. Remember how my father used to vanish?" Her hands waved like birds. "Just pick up and go, no word, and reappear six months later, sometimes with a new wound or a tattoo or whatever? I think that warped something in my head. I can't let someone leave without them telling me why."

Bill tensed as he thought about Fiona's father: wiry and tough, with eyes like chips of stone and a shoulder-heavy walk that broadcast he was always ready for violence. "Where's your Dad right now? If he's close. Maybe he can help."

Fiona laughed. "Yeah, and after he killed everyone threatening us, he'd probably take a few potshots at you, just for old times' sake."

Bill remembered how the last family meeting ended. So did his left knee, which sparkled with phantom pain. "I don't get why he doesn't like me. I always tried to be nice to him."

"Yeah, and you both love the same pretentious suits and cars and stuff." Reaching over, Fiona patted his hand. "I've tried telling him that you're a sweet guy, but he doesn't buy it."

Bill took her hand and held it. "Maybe it's because you said I'm sweet."

"I don't understand."

"Your Dad is the ultimate hard-ass. He probably wants you to have a boyfriend who can kill four people with a teacup."

"Next time you see him, tell him you decapitated that dude with a Tesla. He'll be real impressed."

"That was out of character for me."

"You killed that sheriff in the farmhouse."

"Well, you massacred all his deputies. Along with that Elvis guy."

Fiona winced. "I feel bad about that. About Elvis, at least."

Bill chose his words carefully. "You can't predict what people will do. You were just trying to protect us."

She sighed. "I hope so."

On the intercom screen, the Dean waved a hand at two of his men, who disappeared into the weed forest. Something was afoot.

"I was serious about calling your Dad," Bill said.

"Why?"

"Because he can kill four people with a pencil. Besides, it's better than just sitting here, waiting for them to cut their way in."

Fiona shook her head. "There are other people we can try. Simon, maybe. He likes money. He hates the Dean."

Bill read her face. "You're scared."

"A little bit, yeah. I haven't called my Dad for help since I was a teenager. It makes me uncomfortable."

"You know what else will make you uncomfortable?"

"Those guys outside shooting us full of holes?"

"That's right. Calling him, it's a fantastic idea, if I do say so myself."

Fiona stood and tossed a block of money into the center of the room. She repeated that process with another million dollars, and then another, until she had a platform of cash roughly four feet high. "Don't get full of yourself or anything," she said, stepping onto it. "I once found you dangling from a gantry by your ankles."

Bill snorted. "That little bartender knocked me out."

"A likely story." Fishing a coin from her pocket, Fiona loosened the two screws holding the ceiling vent in place. After handing the vent to Bill, she pulled out her phone and extended it into the shaft as far as her arm could reach, the lit screen tilted toward her. If the phone was outside the panic room's concrete shell, it might catch a bit of signal…

Please give me some good luck today.

The phone flashed one bar. She almost yelped with joy.

"It work?" Bill asked, his voice rising with hope.

"Maybe," she said, dialing a number she knew by heart. It rang, and she tapped the speaker button. Come on, she thought. For the first time in years, I need you, so pick up, pick up, pick up—

A click, followed by a voice deep and rumbling as a rockslide. "Yeah?"

Relief washed through her, so heady she laughed. "Dad?"

"Kiddo?"

"Yeah," she said. "Hey, listen, where are you?"

"If you're still in New York, closer than you think," he

said. "Bill with you?"

"Hey, Walker," Bill called out. "How's it going?"

"Fine, Bill. Kiddo, let's get to it. You're in trouble. I saw on the news."

"We're in a panic room," Fiona said. "My former boss is outside. They can't get in, but we can't stay here forever."

"What's the address?"

She rattled it off. "It's a building under construction. Top floor. There are a lot of men here."

"Not the worst problem." Walker chuckled. "You armed?"

"Yeah, with barely a pop gun."

"Still better than no gun. Hold tight, I'm on my way."

"Why are you here?"

"What?"

"In the city?"

"I just said: I saw you on the news. Figured you needed the help. Plus, it gave me an excuse to leave Canada. It's boring up there, and not always in a good way."

"Well, we're glad you're here."

"So am I, sweetie. How's your battery life?"

"Twenty percent."

"Then turn it off. Call me back in forty-five minutes. Got it?"

"Got it."

"See you soon."

Withdrawing her hand from the shaft, Fiona powered the phone down. She debated whether to reattach the vent. No, she would just need to unscrew it again. Besides, maybe leaving it open would drain off some of this sticky heat.

Bill held out a hand, escorting her from atop the money pile. "That was lucky," he said.

"Oh yeah. It'd been awhile."

"When we were down in Cuba, you didn't try ringing him up?"

Fiona slipped the weapon into her waistband. "Truthfully, I did. Once. He didn't pick up. He gets weird sometimes, disappears to this place in northern Quebec. It's like a retreat for old spies, someplace they can hang out and drink, fight over who set up the most coups or whatever."

"Maybe we should have run there."

"No chance. Very exclusive. You need at least four former dictators in your phone contacts to get in. I'm kidding, but sort of not."

"And your Dad hates me, so there's that."

"You're just not his type, but that's okay." Fiona kissed him on the cheek. "What matters is, you're my type."

Bill kissed her forehead before turning to the intercom screen. The Dean stood in the middle of the floor, his hands on his hips, chin upturned, dramatically lit by grow-lights. He looked like a bronze statue to assholedom, something you'd set up in a park for the dogs to piss on. What was he waiting for?

Something rattled in the ceiling. Fiona stepped away from the vent, her hand skimming her pistol-grip. Her nostrils flared, scenting vomit. No, it was a different smell: acrid, almost like a burning. She knew it well, and adrenaline spiked her blood. As Bill retreated against the wall, she grabbed one of the water-cooler jugs and dragged into the center of the room. Her fingers tore at the thick plastic covering the neck, not finding a grip, slipping. The rattling overhead louder now, the smell beginning to sting her eyes.

"We can toss it out," Bill said, reaching for the red button.

"No," she snapped, her fingernails biting into the plastic, peeling it away.

The tear gas grenade dropped through the open vent, trailing a glossy stream of smoke.

Fiona snatched it in midair. The metal hot, burning her

fingers, as she stuffed it down the neck of the jug. It splashed into the water, and she lifted her leg and slammed her heel over the opening. Her eyes throbbing now, tears frying her cheeks, her throat shut tight. Panic clawing in her skull, yelling at her to run, scream, cry.

"Oh shit," Bill said, coughing and sneezing as he lifted another jug away from the wall.

Water will deactivate the tear gas, she wanted to say, only her throat refused to open. She forced herself to take a slow breath, ignoring how it made her chest burn.

Then another inhale.

Then another.

You're okay. You'll make it.

Bill had the plastic torn off the second jug, and she bent forward so he could pour water over her face, the blessed coolness sweeping away the snot and tears and drool.

"Oh baby, that was the coolest thing," Bill murmured.

She stuck her hands beneath the waterfall pouring from her head, to wash the gas particles away. From the way her fingers ached, the grenade had left burns. Her breaths came a little easier now, but she knew from past experience her lungs would burn for hours. Just another injury for the ledger. At least her vision had cleared to a crimson murk.

Beneath her heel, the grenade had turned the water milky. "Tape," she croaked, pointing to the metal box, and Bill scrambled for it. After they mummified the top of the jug with duct tape, she stepped away. She plucked an energy drink from the stash and drained it, hating the taste but loving how it soothed her throat.

"Where'd you learn to do that?" Bill asked, awed.

"Tulsa," she said. Dispatched by the Dean to solve a problem with a rival, Fiona had found herself in the middle of a riot sparked by a police shooting. From the roof of a burnt-out store, she had watched as protesters dragged plastic water-barrels to the front line and dunked every incoming tear-gas canister.

She said: "How do I look? Fantastic?"

They regarded each other. Fiona with her red eyes and swollen cheeks, her skin stippled with cuts, her body crooked from aches and pains. Bill with his bruised face and bloody knuckles, his front teeth loose, his collar crusted with snot and tears. There was no doubt in Fiona's mind that they shared enough contusions, small fractures, and low-grade organ damage to make a medical billing clerk salivate.

"If we have to go to the ER," Bill said, "we're going to win Patients of the Week."

"At least we have the cash to pay for it." Tossing the empty energy-drink bottle into the corner, she opened a second one and chugged it. Her feet splashed in an inch of water as she walked over to the intercom and hit the button.

"Missed us, fuckers," she boomed into the weed forest, and had the immense pleasure of watching the Dean shake his fists.

The vent must connect to the roof, where the Dean had sent at least one of his men. She bet they wouldn't drop down a fragmentation grenade, but they might try another round of tear gas or pepper spray if the siege dragged on too long. We need to go on offense, Fiona thought, before they hit us again.

"I have a good idea for getting us out of here," she told Bill, pulling out her phone. "But I'm warning you now, it's also pretty damn sick."

15

WALKER ROLLED OUT A BLANKET on the gravel rooftop and knelt down, pulling the rifle-parts from his bag. He fumbled a little when assembling the weapon. He estimated the range at one-fifty yards, light wind. Through the scope he saw people silhouetted against the plastic sheeting that stretched around the inner perimeter of the tower floor, their shapes bulky and spiked in ways that suggested body armor, armaments, serious firepower. Frantic movement, a hoarse shout lost in the wind moaning off the river.

What had Fiona told him once about her employers? They shot first, asked questions last. Fierce types. That was okay, actually. Aggression could be turned against itself, like a rabid dog chewing its own legs.

On the walk from his apartment to the rooftop Walker had stopped in a fast-food place on Vernon to purchase a large soda with fries. To an outsider it might have seemed callous, stopping for snacks while his child sat in a panic room surrounded by armed men, but he trusted Fiona to keep everything locked down until he assessed the situation. If he wanted to stay useful, he needed the calories.

The lights reflecting off the sheeting blocked his view of the interior. He needed to wait for his moment. Flat on his stomach, eye to the scope, he tried to settle into the blanket as best he could, gravel biting his elbows and knees through the thin fabric. When was the last time he had fired this rifle at a human being? Managua?

In addition to the long-gun, he had a pistol with a silencer in the rifle bag, and enough ammunition to last him all night, if things came to that. As much as he had enjoyed his little self-imposed exile up north, the ritual of assembling his armory had activated a deep and pleasurable circuit in his head. He imagined that a chef preparing for a long dinner shift, or a monk squaring away the temple for morning services, felt much the same way.

On the gravel beside him, his phone rang. He tapped the screen without shifting his eye from the scope, expecting to hear Fiona. But the voice that filled his earbud was unwelcome.

"Hey," Sully said. "We're in the city, thought we'd swing by, have a chat."

"You know the first rule of threatening people, Sully?" Walker helped himself to a fry.

Sully snarled: "You're always saying I'm threat—"

"The first rule is, you don't do it," Walker said, talking over him. "If you're going to do someone harm, you don't warn them, first. I used to think you were such a smart guy, when you're really just another punk. What do you want?"

"Just a talk, dude. We can work things out."

Walker shifted his gaze to the phone, extended a finger to end the call. Stopped. "You know what? I'll take you up on that."

"Okay?" Sully sounded surprised. "Where you at?"

Walker gave him the address and hung up. That paranoid bastard would expect some sort of trap, of course, but that was okay. A long time ago, in the jungle, Walker had learned to treat confusion as one of his best friends.

Another five minutes passed. His phone buzzed. Fiona had always been a very punctual girl. "Hey," he said, his finger skimming the rifle's trigger.

"You in position?" All business, that one. Just like her old man.

"Got overwatch, sweetie. What's your play?"

"Loud. Soon as you see anything, if you could start killing everyone in sight, that'd be a big help, okay?"

"Okay. There's something going on in there. Lots of guys running around. I can't quite tell what they're doing, but probably nothing good." For the first time, he wondered how much cover the edge of the roof would provide if these guys shot back at him.

"Just be ready," she said, and clicked off.

On the street below, a black sedan with a smashed front fender cruised at walking pace. Walker shifted and tracked it with the rifle, but the angle made it impossible to see the driver. The sedan squealed to a stop in front of the construction site. From his elevated position, Walker could see the double-wide trailer behind the site's front gate, and the guard who stepped onto its small porch with a submachine gun in his hand.

The driver must have spied the guard through the gate, because the sedan roared forward, its tires leaving faint drifts of smoke. Walker heard its engine echoing off the buildings as it disappeared into the neighborhood. The guard shrugged and headed back inside.

So that was interesting. Who was this other player?

16

FIONA REGRETTED HANGING UP so fast. Given everything that might happen, a part of her wondered if she should have offered more of a goodbye, something heartfelt, in case something happened. But that had never been her relationship with her father: they never had to say the words. They just knew.

It wasn't quite time for fireworks yet. Sitting back, popping bullets from her magazine into her lap, Fiona remembered the heist, five years before, that had put her in a panic room almost exactly like this one. The big difference: instead of sex dolls and energy bars, that room had held a Modigliani painting, along with some mighty fine watches and dusty Civil War antiques. The Dean had wanted the painting ("Not that I particularly like Modigliani, that bohemian caricature," he had told her, "but an asset is an asset…"), so Fiona had broken in, tied up the owner in the kitchen, and snatched the painting.

In short, a perfect job: fast, efficient, painless for everyone except the insurance company. On the way out of the panic room, she had grabbed a timepiece from the shelf: the Piaget Altiplano that still sat on Bill's wrist, thin and precise and beautiful. Almost as good as a wedding ring, as far as she was concerned. Emphasis on *almost*.

"Speaking hypothetically," Bill said behind her, "if I unleashed an enormous fart, do you think it would linger in here?"

Love is a weird thing, Fiona thought. An evolutionary trait, maybe, guaranteeing that we don't kill our mates before we have a chance to reproduce.

"It's not going to matter," she said.

"Why?" Bill asked, looking concerned.

"Because we're leaving." Standing, Fiona slammed the magazine into the pistol and walked over to the bicycle beside the pallet. She pushed it free and stood on the pedals, bouncing to test the wheels. It would roll, and that was all that mattered.

"Hold off, Sundance. We have a problem," Bill said, pointing at the intercom screen, which framed the Dean standing in the open space between the weed forest and the panic room. The Dean gestured at a figure kneeling on the concrete before him. Despite the screen's low resolution, Fiona could see the figure's fine suit shredded, his hair a messy tangle, his face black with injury.

"Oh, Simon," Fiona sighed, climbing off the bicycle. Her stomach felt like an elevator car with the cables cut, plunging for the basement.

The Dean tapped his ear, indicating they should listen in.

Bill swiveled past her to hit the intercom button.

"I'm going to deny my usual impulse to speak at length," the Dean said, "and just put it like this: either you come out, or I'm going to exsanguinate dear Simon here."

Bill released the button. "What's that mean?"

"They're going to kill him," Fiona said, and bit her lower lip.

"I got that part. What's 'exsanguinate' mean?"

It was so tempting to hit Bill, until Fiona remembered that he had met Simon a grand total of twice, briefly. There was no way that Bill would ever understand Simon's grand bullshit sessions, and how she could sit with a barely repressed grin as he tried to pick apart her brain, lighting a fresh cigarette every few questions. Bill never had good mentors.

"It means you bleed out," Fiona said, and took a deep breath. She was sick of killing, sure, but she was going to make an exception for the Dean. In fact, choking him out would put a nice little cap on her murder career.

"What do we do?" Bill squeezed her shoulder.

Pushing Bill's hand away, Fiona pressed the intercom button and held it. *"Simon,"* her voice boomed across the floor. *"Don't give that prissy intellectual any satisfaction, okay?"*

Simon turned his battered face to the ceiling. They had taken his signature sunglasses. The graininess of the intercom screen made it hard to see, but he may have winked. Fiona would have expected nothing less.

The Dean snapped his fingers, and one of the mercs walked over with a wicked blade, offered handle-first.

17

WALKER'S EAR BUZZED, and he answered: "Yeah."

"Do it," Fiona said, sounding tense.

Walker tucked into the rifle, eye slotted to the scope. "What am I firing at?" Shadows jumped and merged behind the plastic. "I can't see shit."

"Doesn't matter," she said, and through Walker's earpiece Walker came a faint crackling. "Just need the noise. Now. Please."

Walker's finger tightened on the trigger. He found a half-way suitable target—a dark splotch that looked like a giant with a machete—and took a deep breath. Held it. Exhaled, and pulled.

18

THE DEAN'S FINGERS HAD BARELY touched the handle of the merc's offered blade when the merc's head exploded, ruining the Dean's suit.

The other mercs, acting on instinct, dove for the concrete, their weapons already unslung. One spied the hole in the plastic that marked the trajectory of Walker's bullet, and fired off a burst that converted a thousand dollars' worth of prime weed into a spray of leaves, stems and dirt.

That was all it took: everyone else with a weapon pulled its trigger, unleashing a storm of lead that shredded the plastic sheeting. Bullets sparked off concrete and steel, echoing into the night.

The Dean wiped a moist sleeve across his face, clearing his eyes, and looked around for Simon. That damn philistine had scrambled off somewhere, probably cowering behind a pillar while the Dean's men decided to wreck this entire harvest.

Retrieving the blade from the floor, the Dean stalked after

his prey—but only made it three feet before the panic room door slid open, revealing something that left him, the most prolix of men, utterly speechless for the first time in his life.

19

BILL KNEW HOW PLANS could implode.

Years ago, as a favor he quickly regretted, Bill had offered to stage-manage the robbery of a bank vault loaded with a hundred million dollars in precious diamonds. It was a little heavier than his usual scams, but the Dean had faith in Bill's abilities to wrangle a group of psychotic idiots. The vault was protected by the latest in technology: thermal and light sensors, as well as a set of large magnetic plates around the three-foot-thick door. If anyone tried to enter the vault without inputting a twelve-digit code into the keypad, the opening door would break the magnetic field produced by the plates, summoning every cop for two hundred miles around.

Bill found three men with the know-how for the job: an old-school Lock Picker who could, with the aid of his trusty stethoscope and a few other tools, suss out the combination of the vault lock; a punky Kid with some experience in alarms and traps; and a Lunatic who could handle the magnetic plates. Bill's internal warning system, usually so fine-tuned, should have blared when the Lunatic raised his bandaged hands and announced that he had embedded magnets under the skin of his palms, the better to sense the magnetic fields. The rhythms of the galaxy, the man called it. Whatever.

The night of the robbery, things commenced smoothly. Bill sat in a car parked across the street from the bank, the police scanner on the dashboard blissfully silent, sipping the world's worst cup of takeout coffee. From the phone on the seat beside him came the Lock Picker's voice, narrating their progress. With his tingling hands, the Lunatic had duct-taped custom magnets to each of the magnetic plates, keeping the field intact. The Lock Picker had cracked the combination, and the Kid was using hairspray and towels to disable the sensors inside the dark vault.

Even as he mainlined caffeine, Bill felt his body begin to relax. In addition to the diamonds, the lockboxes in the vault supposedly held all manner of ledgers, illicit photos, and blackmail material—more than enough to fuel Bill's projects for the next year or two.

Over the phone, someone began screaming.

Bill shot upright, lukewarm coffee drenching his designer jeans. Over a loud boom, he heard the Lunatic shriek about the rhythms and power of the universe, and he knew the job had gone totally to shit. Bill slapped the glove compartment until it popped open, revealing a small pistol he always tucked there just in case. Then he was out of the car, running toward the bank just as the Kid and the Lock Picker burst through the front doors, bags over their shoulders, their faces hard with panic. They barely made the sidewalk before the bank exploded with harsh light and alarms, loud enough to pulverize Bill's eardrums into a quaking mess.

They dove into the car, Bill fumbling for the ignition

as the Lock Picker screamed something about the Lunatic knocking the magnets free and retreating into the vault, ready to meet God. Maybe all those magnets under his skin had screwed with his nerves, but whatever the case, the entire operation was toast. Bill hit the gas and headed for the Queens-Midtown Tunnel, praying that the Dean wouldn't kill any of them for screwing this up.

The police arrested the Lunatic, who confessed only to wanting to touch the face of the Almighty. Less than five hours later, someone drove a pencil through his neck in a holding cell. And the next morning, the Dean assigned Bill to the Sea Shack, that little restaurant on the rougher end of Rockaway Beach, where he could run his blissfully lower-key scams in peace.

So Bill could tell you all about things going haywire.

Like Fiona's plan, for instance.

How the hell had he agreed to *this* insanity?

The answer was obvious: they had no choice.

20

AS SOON AS FIONA ENDED THE CALL with her father, she smacked the big red button that opened the panic room. The door groaned inward, plowing a small wave of murky water over their feet. A bullet sparked off the steel frame and angled into the room, exploding into a box of energy bars, and Bill ducked with a yelp. Fiona dug her heels into the wet concrete, gripped the bike seat, and pushed with all her might.

That exertion made every muscle in her back scream bloody murder, her knees quake, her head throb—but it was all worth it when the bike hissed out of the panic room, gaining a bit of speed on the slight downslope, the sex doll in the saddle already spurting black smoke from its eyes and mouth. By the time it reached the weed forest, the flares and fireworks that Fiona had stuffed into its unmentionables had begun to cook off, red and yellow sparks vomiting from its mouth. Its prim blue pantsuit burst into flames.

The Dean, along with every merc, turned their collective head to watch the abomination cycle past, bubbling and popping.

Fiona leveled her pistol, ready to use this precious instant of distraction to take out as many of these bastards as possible.

That was all according to plan.

What happened next, though, was decidedly not.

The bicycle veered into the line of chemical barrels lining one side of the floor. Bill grabbed Fiona's shoulder and yanked her to the floor as the world flashed white. A storm of flaming weed scraps burst through the gap in the door, sprinkling their backs, as the water around them frothed from the shockwave. Bill's ears popped.

The exterior camera had miraculously survived the explosion. On the intercom screen, Bill saw the bicycle and its plastic rider dissolve into a pillar of flame, screamers and streamers and dazzlers rocketing through space, as the flickering figures of the surviving mercs tried to take cover.

"Think you used enough dynamite there, Butch?" Bill yelled.

"Shut up and get your bag," Fiona hissed. In between wiring up the doll and talking with her father, she had mummified the wrecked duffel bag with the entire roll of duct tape, hopefully making it strong enough to hold all the paper money and gold they had stuffed inside it.

Gritting his teeth, Bill lifted the bag onto his shoulder, and Fiona slid through the doorway into the smoky chaos beyond. The floor was a disaster, coated with dirt and ash and leaves and sliding wet bits. The plastic sheeting torn to shreds. A merc stood to her left, raising a pistol, but before Fiona could squeeze off a shot the right side of his chest exploded, filling the air with pink mist, and he fell.

His tumbling form revealed another merc, who varied from all the other dead and dying men on the floor only by the red bandana wrapped around the lower part of his face.

This one managed to lift his AR-15 maybe a foot before the top of his head vaporized.

Fiona was sensing a pattern here.

"Thanks, Dad," she muttered, switching her pistol for the rifle, crouching so she could check the magazine. Fully loaded. Rising, she swept the zone, low and cautious. She passed the doll, reduced to a sludge of bubbling plastic and blackened cardboard atop a pair of pockmarked legs, the bicycle twisted into a black pretzel.

The far end of the floor was a wall of fire, crisping plants, melting plastic, feeding on the scattered bodies. The heat needled her skin. She swept from pillar to pillar, hoping that her father could see well enough through the smoke to cover her back from his faraway perch. Where were Simon and the Dean?

Over the crackle of flames, she heard rumbling machinery. Of course. Moving faster, she angled toward the construction elevator, her traitorous throat itching as she inhaled lungfuls of aerosolized weed, mercs, and plastic. She coughed into an upraised elbow, hoping the sound was lost in the chaos, and approached the edge of the floor. Through the flickering smog she glimpsed the unmistakable figure of the Dean, his arm tight around Simon's neck as he limped toward the open elevator door.

Edging behind the nearest pillar, she called out: "Stop."

The Dean spun, digging a small silver automatic into Simon's chest, near the heart. Simon's cheeks were marked with a dozen rough cuts, his eyes swollen, his hair a gray tangle—but when he saw Fiona, he offered a wolf's smile.

Fiona squinted, judging angles. On a good day, with no injuries, she might have tried to hit the small sliver of the Dean's face she could see over Simon's shoulder. But the rifle trembled in her grip, the iron sights wavering, her eyes watering. Could her Dad see them? Probably not—he would have risked the shot.

"Let him go," Fiona said.

"And then what, you'll let me go?" The Dean laughed. "Not bloody likely, dear."

Fiona sensed Bill limping behind her, and twitched her head to the right: circle around me. He entered her peripheral vision, hunched beneath the weight of the money bag, aiming a pistol with stiff arms. She really would have to teach him proper stance someday.

"A steady return," the Dean said, and took another step backward, pulling Simon with him. "And you had to ruin it."

"Say what?" Fiona took a step forward, mirroring his movement.

"We had a simple goal, my associates and I." Another step. "Provide a steady return for our investors. Profit by any means possible. No different from your typical corporate board, understand?"

"Regular companies don't use bullets," Bill offered.

"Their loss." The Dean's eyes darted between Bill and Fiona, judging which might fire first. "A gun really speeds up negotiations."

Simon sighed and rolled his eyes.

"You should have left us alone," Bill said. "The money I stole from you, kicking this whole thing off, you wouldn't have missed it."

"It wasn't about the money, you ignoramus," the Dean sputtered. "It was about the *principle*."

Simon sighed louder. "Blah, blah, blah," he said, and, quick as a viper, reached up and grabbed the barrel of the Dean's pistol. The Dean pulled the trigger on reflex, but Simon already had the firearm angled up. The bullet plowed through the Dean's head, coating the walls of the construction elevator with all his esoteric knowledge. No great loss.

21

"**WELL, THAT WAS FRIGGIN' IMPRESSIVE,**" Fiona said, as they stood over the dead body of the Dean, which had toppled into the elevator doorway. The Dean's final expression was a snarl of extreme disgust.

"You have catlike reflexes, Simon." Bill stuffed his pistol into his waistband and bent to loot the Dean's pockets. "If you were ever part of a ping-pong league, you'd dominate. You should totally think about it."

Simon turned to Fiona. "Does he ever shut up?"

Fiona laughed. "No. And that's what I love about him."

From the Dean's inner pocket, Bill extracted an unsmoked cigar, examining its label in the firelight. "Cuban. Looking forward to smoking this."

Simon snapped his fingers. "That's mine. For reasons it would take too long to explain. Give it here."

With a theatrical frown, Bill handed the cigar over, and Simon slipped it into his mouth. "Fiona, you owe me some money," he said, as he pulled a gold lighter from his wrecked suit. "How much is in Bill's bag?"

"Maybe a million in currency," Fiona said. "And a lot of gold chunks."

Simon lit the tip of the cigar and puffed a velvety cloud. "I will take some of those chunks and leave you the rest. You are getting a significant discount, for saving my life, and for helping me take care of our friend here. He killed most of my men, but I have enough left to rebuild."

"Done," Fiona said, shooting Bill a warning glance before he could protest.

Shifting the cigar into the corner of his mouth, Simon walked over to the bag, which Bill had dropped at the foot of the closest pillar, and unzipped it. After a bit of rummaging, he returned with two lumps of gold in his right hand, the tendons in his forearm straining with the weight. "Quite the balls," he announced.

"That's what she said," Bill offered.

"I am going to take this car down, alone," Simon said, kicking the Dean's ribs until the body flopped into the elevator. "The Dean and I have a bit of business to conduct. A little bit of *quid pro quo* for my rug. Do not ask."

"I'll see you around," Fiona said.

Simon hit a button, and the grating rattled shut. "Always up for a chat," he called, unzipping his fly with his free hand as the elevator rumbled out of sight.

"I don't want to know what he's going to do," Bill said, hefting the duffel. "Shall we take the stairs down? I don't really want to wait for the elevator to come back up, considering the whole building's burning."

"Good idea," she said, pulling out her phone and dialing.

Walker picked up on the first ring. "How's it going, you crazy kids?"

"We're coming down." She slung the rifle onto her back.

"The Dean's dead."

"Make it snappy," Walker said, all business. "I'm heading down to the street."

"On the way." As they trotted for the stairs on the far side of the floor, they passed the charred remains of Crow Man, an oversized joint still clutched in his blackened hand. She plucked the joint free, slipped it in her mouth, and bent her head to the oily flames snaking up a nearby pillar.

"Really?" Bill asked. "Really?"

Sweaty Fiona inhaled deep, held it, and blew a smoke ring. "It's been a long day."

Shaking his head, Bill resumed his zombie-like shuffle for the stairwell. Fiona took another puff before returning the joint to Crow Man's crisped grasp. It seemed like an appropriate gesture. There was too much adrenaline in her blood for the weed to mellow her out, but she hoped the chemicals would ease the pain in her joints until they could reach a real doctor.

Bill was waiting at the exit door, his back to her. She tapped him on the shoulder: "Come on, move."

"Can't," he said, and when she peeked around him, she saw the reason why: on the lower flight stood a young woman in an oversized nylon jacket. Her hair was tied back in a tight blonde ponytail, her face a bloodless mask in the dimness of the stairwell. She pointed a pistol at them, her hand steady.

Bill said: "Hello, Casey."

22

THE PISTOL IN CASEY'S HAND trembled a little. It might have been a trick of the firelight behind them, but Fiona swore she saw a tear glinting on the woman's cheek. Fiona's hand skimmed the rifle-strap across her shoulders, but Bill was blocking any shot she could take. Damn.

"Back up," Fiona whispered in Bill's ear, thinking: I guess Dad left his sniper post a little too early. Would've been great to have him send a high-velocity round through this bitch's ear.

As they retreated through the doorway, Bill tossed the duffel bag aside. "Throw your guns, too." Casey said, waving the pistol. With two fingers, Fiona lifted the strap from her shoulder and lowered her rifle to the floor. Moving in slow motion, Bill reached into his waistband, lifted out his pistol by the grip, and tossed it away.

The flames had reached the nearest row of weed plants, which popped and sizzled, the heat baking the back of Fiona's neck. The sight of the burning forest made Casey hesitate in the doorway. "The hell is this place?"

"Belonged to our old boss," Bill said.

Casey wiped the sweat from her forehead. "Same guys you were running from?"

"Yeah," Fiona said, pulling Bill after her. If they retreated, gave this girl a little space, they might have more options. "Why are you here?"

Casey's lips wavered, along with her gun-hand. "Why do you think?"

"We killed your family?" Bill offered.

"Yes," Casey said. "It took me so long to find you…"

"You hit us in the car. On the highway." Fiona circled wide, away from the fires, tugging Bill. Over the rumble of the dying building, they heard the shriek of distant sirens.

"Yes. I took a shot at you, too," Casey said. "At the vet?"

Fiona remembered crashing through the front door of that Oklahoma farmhouse and finding Casey on the couch, a girl crushed under the weight of her family history. The girl who fled into the night, rather than fight and kill with the rest of her clan. "You're a good tracker," Fiona said. "I admire that."

"Stop moving," Casey said, raising the gun an inch.

Fiona took another step back, and stopped. They were five feet from the edge of the building, the wind snapping at her hair. A storm of orange sparks drifted past, flickering, gone. She gripped a handful of Bill's shirt and tugged to the right, slightly, positioning him.

"Casey," Bill said. "Can you tell my girlfriend here that we didn't do anything in that bar? That you just knocked me out?"

"Hush," Fiona whispered in his ear.

The barrel of the pistol loomed as large as a highway tunnel as Casey came closer, her eyes unleashing the full waterworks, tears dripping off her chin. "I know my people did you wrong," she sniffed. "I do. But blood is blood."

"I'm sorry we killed them," Fiona said. "I'd like to think they understood."

"Okay then." Casey nodded, and her finger drifted over the safety and hammer of the pistol, making sure everything was set properly. She took a deep breath. "Okay."

Before Casey's finger could find the trigger, Fiona braced her hands against Bill's back and shoved as hard as she could, sending her boyfriend toppling into Casey's knees. Casey fell backward, her pistol clattering away. Squawking Bill scrambled after the weapon, and Fiona leapt over him to grab a handful of Casey's jacket.

Casey thrashed, but Fiona was having none of it tonight. She lifted Casey into the air and spun, Casey's boots scraping the edge of the abyss. Every muscle in Fiona's arms burned like the forest behind them. It would have been so easy to loosen her grip, to let the night have this damaged soul. And yet she held fast.

"I'm sorry," Casey said.

"You're fine," Fiona said through gritted teeth, although nothing about this situation was fine at all. "You still have choices."

"Sure." Casey let her head flop back, scanning the ground so far below.

Fiona's arms quivered as she shifted, dragging Casey a foot to the left. "In this life, there's no safe harbor, okay? Remember that, and you'll be fine. When you wake up, get away from the building."

"When I…" Casey's eyes widened.

"Sorry." Fiona tossed her.

Bill rolled to the edge in time to witness Casey crash through four debris nets bolted to the building exterior—slowing her fall considerably—before she landed on a huge pile of sand beside the lobby doors. "Think she'll ever walk again?" he asked.

"Hey, I was gentle." Fiona returned to the duffel bag. Hopefully they wouldn't need to carry this damn thing much longer. Her AR-15 would be a little too conspicuous once they reached the street, so she took Casey's pistol from Bill and shoved it down the back of her jeans.

"Did you mean what you said?" Bill asked.

"About no safe harbor?" Fiona jutted her chin at the streets far below, frantic with colored lights as an army of fire trucks converged on the building. "There's none for us, if we don't get out of here right now."

23

A BURNING TABLE SMASHED into the dumpsters to their right, lighting the way as Fiona and Bill trotted for the rear fence. Neither looked back as the top two floors of the building vaporized in a cloud of fire and dust, and a pillar of fragrant smoke rose into the night sky. Crow Man would have been proud: by morning, half of western Queens had a contact high from his final batch of weed.

On the sidewalk, they headed left, away from the fire-trucks screaming for the construction site's front gate. The first responders from the NYPD would likely arrive in minutes, and if they blocked off the surrounding streets, that would create some real problems. What do you say if a cop sees your clothes splattered with blood, your face covered in ash, and a bag filled with crisp hundred-dollar bills on your back? *Oh yeah, just out for a stroll, officer. By the way, I have a really big gun.*

As they scurried across the intersection, her phone buzzed. Fiona pushed Bill into the cover of a warehouse doorway and answered it.

"Where are you?" Walker asked.

"A block away," she said. "You got a car?"

The brick wall across the street flickered blue and red. A siren chirped. The growing roar of a powerful engine. The first cop had arrived.

"Yeah," Walker said. "I got a car."

"There's a warehouse to the north of the construction site," Fiona said, trying to press further into the shadows, Bill's breath loud in her other ear. "We're in the doorway, but it's a crappy hiding place."

The police cruiser appeared, slowing at the intersection. Its spotlight played over the road, the fence, the wall to their right. Behind her, Bill rattled the doorknob. "Locked," he whispered.

The spotlight hit the doorway, so bright they had to squint. Fiona readied for the megaphoned voice telling them to step out, place their hands on their heads, get on their knees. She had the pistol, of course, but hated the idea of shooting a cop who wasn't crooked.

"There you are," Walker shouted out the cruiser's open window. "Come on, what are you waiting for?"

"Is that you?" Fiona stepped out of the doorway, raising a hand to shield her eyes. The brightness made it impossible to see the figure behind the wheel.

"No, it's Santa Claus." Walker sounded impatient. "I borrowed a cop car. Come on."

"When I was three, you told me Santa Claus didn't exist," Fiona yelled.

"Just preparing you for the real world, baby. Bill, come on."

Grinning Bill had already trotted past her to open the front passenger door. He stepped aside and bowed, ushering her into the seat. She saw her father behind the wheel, silhouetted by the smoky glow of the burning building, and remembered that long-ago night in Delaware, when he had come to save her at the mall.

"Describe this 'borrow a cop car' thing," she said, ducking into the front seat with the bag in her lap. Bolted to the dashboard was a stack of radios and a computer screen in a thick plastic frame. Between that and the canvas rifle-bag stuffed into her footwell, she found it a tough squeeze.

"Cop car stopped right in front of the building where I was." Walker tapped a command on the keyboard built into the console between their seats, and the screen displayed lines of dispatch codes. "Two officers. I didn't kill them, don't worry. I left them cuffed and gagged."

"Good to see you, sir," Bill said from the backseat. "Can we get out of here?"

"Pretty boy, you look like shit," Walker said, and activated the siren. The cruiser had a real beast of an engine: when he stomped on the gas, it went from zero to light-speed in under three seconds. At the next intersection, he did some fast wheel-work, cornering hard enough to press Fiona against her window.

That would have been the one good thing about becoming a cop, Fiona mused. You could drive like this with impunity, never worrying about someone pulling you over. Back when I was a teenager, and took that officer's car, I should have spent a little more time behind the wheel, squeeze some extra fun out of it. Then again, if I'd done that, they would have arrested me, and my life would have worked out totally different. Maybe in some alternate universe, I'm working in an office somewhere, bored out of my skull.

"You okay?" Walker asked.

"Feeling nostalgic," she said. "Remember that time I

ended up in that mall, and you had to come and get me?"

"Sure," he said. "Probably your most idiotic moment as a kid."

Bill stuck his fingers through the grating that separated the seats, skimming the back of her neck. "What happened?" he asked.

"Nothing," Fiona said. "Doesn't matter. You got a new car lined up, Dad?"

"There's always a car lined up, you have the right tools." He peered through the windshield, scanning the street. He seemed distracted.

"We okay?" Fiona asked.

"Should be. I expected someone else to maybe show up, but no sign of them. Probably for the best." He studied her in the light of the dashboard screen. "You look like you could use a doctor."

"Know anyone good? I have a guy, Trevor, but I think this is a little outside his skillset."

"Trevor, your ex?"

"Yes, my ex-boyfriend."

Walker winked. "Oh yeah, he was great. How's he doing?"

In the backseat, Bill leaned back and sighed, loudly enough for Walker to lock eyes with him in the rearview mirror. "How's it going back there, Bill?" Walker asked. "Comfortable? I know it's not your first time in the backseat of a cruiser."

"Nothing like a cop car," Bill said.

"I got a guy," Walker said, turning to Fiona. "Physician at Mount Sinai, runs a private office on the side, let's say. Limited hours. We can head there once we dump the car. You going to make it?"

Fiona nodded. "Yeah. Thank you, by the way. We wouldn't have made it otherwise."

A raindrop spattered the windshield, then another. Fiona's heart leapt. Nothing like a nighttime storm to make you a little more invisible. She was smiling, about to say something in praise of the weather, when the world exploded in shattered glass and screaming metal.

24

TWO CAR ACCIDENTS IN ONE DAY?

Seriously, what were the odds?

If you're a fugitive on the run, the chances are probably high, although that failed to comfort Fiona as she ran her hands over her body. No wounds, but her guts felt stuffed with ice, making her shiver. That was shock, her old friend, setting up housekeeping.

The police cruiser had flipped upside down, leaving Walker and Fiona suspended by their seatbelts. The cash bag had tumbled to the ceiling, now the floor, along with Walker's rifle bag. She could turn her head enough to see the backseat. Bill was pressed against the grating, bleeding from the head but still conscious.

"Really?" Bill muttered. "Really?"

"Brace yourself," Walker said, placing his hand on her seatbelt release, so she planted her feet on the dashboard and locked her legs. He hit the button, and she let her body sag to the ceiling. As she did, her left side crackled with fresh pain. From her new angle, she could see headlights reflecting through the shattered glass of the passenger windows.

"Who," she said, helping Walker unlock his seatbelt.

Walker's slow somersault ended with them shoulder-to-shoulder. He squinted at the other car. "Friends of mine," he said, turning to yank his door handle. The driver's side door squeaked halfway open before slamming into a parked car. Walker scrambled out, keeping low.

"*Walker,*" someone yelled beyond the headlights. "*We just want to talk.*"

Walker rolled his eyes. "Come on, move."

In the backseat, Bill smacked the handles. "I'm stuck in here," he said, voice high with panic.

"Kick, baby," Fiona said, grabbing Walker's rifle bag by the canvas handle and dragging it after her, over the smashed radios and dashboard screen. The pavement was hard on her elbows as she crawled after Walker, toward the rear of the cruiser. Bill slammed both feet into the window a foot from her face, cracking it into a gummy mess, scattering bits of glass over Walker, who held up a hand and snarled.

"Sorry," Bill said.

"*Fine,*" shouted the voice beyond the light, and Fiona, hearing the metallic click of safeties, gripped Bill by the ankles and yanked as hard as her bruised muscles allowed, dragging him over broken glass and the window's crumpled sill into the narrow space between two parked vehicles. Walker behind her, on the sidewalk, crouched behind an ultra-compact Smart coupe that looked barely sturdy enough to resist a spitball, much less the fusillade they knew was coming.

It took only ten seconds for five automatic rifles to exhaust their clips, but the explosions seemed to last forever to Fiona, tangled in the gutter with Bill and the rifle bag. Bits of glass and metal rained on them as bullets shredded the parked cars. A stray shot or twelve hit something inside the cruiser, and the siren shrieked before falling silent.

"Who are they?" Fiona hissed at Walker, who had drawn a pistol from his jacket.

"Tell you later," Walker said, inching his head to the window of the coupe. The angle of the headlights made it hard to see much, but he picked out Sully's lanky silhouette on the passenger side of the attacking vehicle. Shadows scurried around him, men finding new positions.

Walker poked his pistol onto the window-sill and fired three times at Sully, who disappeared from view. Another flicker, to his left. Walker shifted and fired again, and this time someone screeched like a rabbit caught in a trap.

Between the parked cars, Fiona felt for the pistol in her waistband. It was missing. Had it slipped out? Was it still in the cruiser?

"Walker," Sully called. "Who's that with you? Your kid? How sweet."

Another burst of rifle-fire chewed the edge of the coupe, sending its crumpled rear fender into the gutter. Walker swiveled his head to examine the street. In the chaos and adrenaline of the crash, he had failed to notice the Queensboro Bridge looming in the distance, its steel and stone lit a sickly yellow, shimmery in the soft rain. They were still in that industrial area of chop-shops and boarded-up warehouses that ran like an ancient vein through the shiny new Queens.

Walker edged his head up and fired again, aiming this time at the headlights. One shattered. He ducked as a burst of automatic fire skipped off the coupe's hood.

"That's the best you got?" Sully sounded closer, somewhere to the left.

Fiona dug into Walker's bag, feeling rifle pieces, no time to assemble, damn. The ringing in her ears had quieted enough for her to hear a dull thud.

"Hey, what's this?" Sully asked.

The explosion transformed Sully's big black car into a Detroit-made skyrocket, rising into the rainy sky on a pillar of fire. It managed to ascend twenty feet before jealous gravity brought it crashing back to earth in a storm of sparks and oily smoke. The overturned police cruiser blocked Fiona, Bill, and Walker from the worst of the flames. Raindrops sizzled into steam on hot metal.

Beneath Fiona, Bill shouted something lost in the ringing aftermath of the explosion.

She shouted back: "What?"

Bill held up his left index finger, ringed with a grenade pin. "Got it off a body when I left the panic room. Put it in the money bag."

Kissing him on the cheek, Fiona rose to a crouch. Despite the chemical smoke stinging her eyes, she could pick out one, two, three bodies scattered on the wet road, none moving. If a big car held five people, that meant two others still alive, maybe.

Walker stood, a two-handed grip on his pistol as he sidestepped from behind the coupe. He had never liked explosives. At least with a gun you knew the direction of force. When you blew something up, all sorts of unexpected things could happen. Even so, whatever Bill had done had tied things up quite nicely.

Three dead bodies, and a big chap trying to crawl toward the darkness on the far side of the street, leaving a black smear behind him. Based on that stupendous amount of blood left on the pavement, Walker guessed the guy had a minute or two before he kicked the bucket. Where was Sully?

"Walker," Sully said.

Walker turned and saw Sully on the far side of the pyre, illuminated by flame, his glorious moustache drooping with rainwater. He had a submachine gun in one hand, barrel pointed down. He was trying to pop in a new magazine, but something was wrong with his other hand, his sleeve gleaming bright with blood. Walker noted the bits of window-glass glittering like diamonds in Sully's cheeks and forehead.

"Just wanted a chat," Sully said, and laughed. It sounded bubbly. The magazine dropped from his hand, clattering off his boot. He looked at it and shrugged.

"Yeah, a friendly chat," Walker said, nodding at the dead men with rifles in their hands.

Sully shrugged, his knees wobbling. "I guess you're not a Fe—"

Walker shot Sully clean through the head and tossed the pistol through the window of the burning car. Without pause, he turned on his heel and walked around the cruiser, finding Bill and Fiona on the sidewalk with their bag of money. "You didn't mention you were carrying around explosives," he said to Bill.

"Be prepared." Bill smiled.

Walker pinched Bill's cheek as he took the rifle bag from Fiona. "Well, I'm glad you showed a little initiative," he said. "You can come kill folks with me anytime."

"Can we get out of here?" Fiona groaned.

"So much for bonding." Walker shouldered his rifle bag and started north, toward the bridge, mulling contingencies. Neither cop had gotten a good look at his face when he stole the cruiser. With any luck, the police would take the path of least resistance and pin the theft on Sully.

Bill and Fiona did their best to keep pace with Walker's loping form, but their wounds made it hard to move at anything close to regular speed. If she put her weight on her right leg, Fiona found, she could limp pretty well. She wanted to ask her father about the dead men back there, but he seemed intent on getting as far from the burning car as possible. For Walker, this was just another Tuesday.

25

BENEATH THE BRIDGE, WALKER paused beside a boxy car that looked older than Fiona, its white flanks spotted with rust, its backseat stuffed with plastic bags and other trash. Walker lifted the rifle bag and drove it hard into the driver's side window, shattering it, before reaching in and unlocking the doors. "Vintage," he told them. "Just like me."

"Positively ancient," Fiona said, climbing into the back with Bill.

Walker slid into the driver's seat and sorted through the junk in the console. "Hey, it's our lucky night," he said, holding up a screwdriver.

As Walker bent to the ignition, stabbing and prying, Bill asked: "Who were those guys?"

"Old friend," Walker said, fiddling with wires. "Got paranoid, thought I was a Fed. He was the one I was trying to lure into a trap, back at that construction site, but he didn't show in time. Too bad he found us after."

The car sputtered to life, its frame shuddering. Walker

flicked on the lights and the windshield wipers. "Where to?"

Where indeed? For the first time in what felt like forever, they had no pursuers. It was an odd sensation, not being hunted. Fiona would need time to get used to it. "Doctor," she said. "Then we're getting out of this damn city, at least for a little while."

Walker nodded, worked the gearshift, and started off. They hit the onramp to the bridge and swept across the East River, toward the bright lights of Manhattan and the darkness of America beyond. The rain came down harder, smearing the world into streaks of color.

Bill leaned into her and asked: "You remember what our friend in Oklahoma told us to do?"

She pressed into him. "Duck or we'll get shot?"

"No, right before the end." His voice lowered. "He said we needed to get married, specifically at a chapel in Vegas."

"You're kidding," she said.

"No, I'm not. You remember." Taking her hand, he slipped the grenade pin over her ring finger.

"Oh shit," Walker groaned, watching them in the rearview mirror.

"Walker, your opinion is noted," Bill said, staring into Fiona's eyes.

"Okay. I mean, yes. Yes, I will." Fiona wiped at her cheeks. "When we make this legal, which fake identities are we going to use on the marriage certificate?"

"We'll make new ones. Fresh start."

"I'm going to be sick," Walker muttered, but he was smiling.

"Careful," Fiona growled, "or I'm not inviting you."

"Well, I already got your wedding present," Walker said. "Thanks to some work I did earlier, the FBI is already off your ass, along with a big chunk of law enforcement. It's not a totally clean slate, but it's probably as close as you're going to get."

"Daddy, you're the best."

Bill settled back in his seat, musing about clean sheets and healed skin, good suits and Fiona pressed warmly against him in the dark. He squeezed Fiona's hand, hard, and she squeezed back. We're safe, he realized. Maybe I don't deserve it, and maybe it's not for long, but we're safe.

Walker hit the off-ramp. As they swept into Manhattan, Bill glimpsed a figure in gleaming white on the sidewalk. It was a man in a rhinestone Elvis costume, hair swept up in a rockabilly pompadour, boots splashing in the puddles as he boogied his heart out. Elvis saw their car and leapt into a wide stance, one hand above his head, the other pointed at them. Thank ya, the gesture said. Thank ya very much.

ACKNOWLEDGMENTS

A COUPLE OF YEARS AGO, when I started what would eventually become "A Brutal Bunch of Heartbroken Saps," the first book in the Love & Bullets trilogy, I had only one publisher in mind: Shotgun Honey, which has perfected the art of the crime-fiction novella. The trilogy owes everything to Ron Earl Phillips. A thousand thanks, Ron. Beers are on me.

NICK KOLAKOWSKI's writing has appeared in *Shotgun Honey*, *McSweeney's Internet Tendency*, *Thuglit*, *The North American Review*, *Spinetingler Magazine*, *Plots with Guns*, and various anthologies. He lives and writes in New York City.

On the following pages are a few
more great titles from the
Down & Out Books publishing family.

For a complete list of books and to
sign up for our newsletter,
go to **DownAndOutBooks.com**.

Boise Longpig Hunting Club
Nick Kolakowski

Down & Out Books
August 2018
978-1-948235-13-6

When you want someone found, you call bounty hunter Jake Halligan. He's smart, tough, and best of all, careful on the job. But none of those skills seem to help him when a shadowy group starts taking his life apart piece by piece…

Boise Longpig Hunting Club is a wild ride into the dark heart of the American dream, where even the most brutal desires can be fulfilled for a price, and nobody is safe from the rich and powerful.

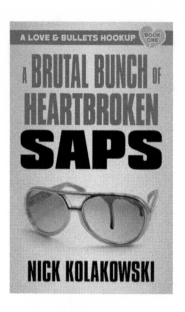

A Brutal Bunch of Heartbroken Saps
A Love & Bullets Hookup
Nick Kolakowski

Shotgun Honey, an imprint of
Down & Out Books
978-1-943402-81-6

Bill is a hustler's hustler with a taste for the high life…who suddenly grows a conscience. However, living the clean life takes a whole lot of money, and so Bill decides to steal a fortune from his employer before skipping town.

Pursued by crooked cops, dimwitted bouncers, and a wisecracking assassin, Bill will need to be a quick study in the way of the gun if he wants to survive his own getaway. Who knew that an honest attempt at redemption could rack up a body count like this?

Slaughterhouse Blues
A Love & Bullets Hookup
Nick Kolakowski

Shotgun Honey, an imprint of
Down & Out Books
978-1-946502-40-7

Holed up in Havana, Bill and Fiona know the Mob is coming for them. But they're not prepared for who the Mob sends: a pair of assassins so utterly amoral and demented, their behavior pushes the boundaries of sanity. Seriously, what kind of killers pause in mid-hunt to discuss the finer points of thread count and luxury automobiles? If they want to survive, our fine young criminals can't retreat anymore: they'll need to pull off a massive (and massively weird) heist—and the loot has some very dark history…

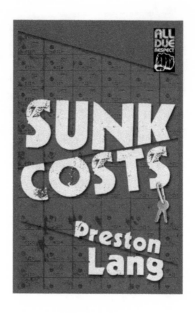

Sunk Costs
Preston Lang

All Due Respect, an imprint of
Down & Out Books
978-1-946502-88-9

Dan is a con man and drifter who thinks he just hitched a ride back east. Instead, he finds himself going 70-miles-an-hour with a gun pointed at his head. But instead of a bullet, he's hit with a proposition to make some fast money. Soon Dan finds himself deeply involved with misdirection, murder, and the sexiest accountant he's ever met.

606286LV00003BA/247/P
LVHW041110402l9
Printed in the USA
at www.ICGtesting.com
CPSIA information can be obtained